Cover design by: Robert Allen

Ripples Across A Pond

Robert Allen

Chapter One
1947

Another cup smashed on the kitchen floor. "Please don't do that Harry, please I'm begging you." Mary Denham stood with her head bowed wringing her hands. She was middle aged but looked a lot older, her hair was prematurely grey and whilst the latest fashion was to have it permed in waves, her's was straight and hung limply on her collar.

Harry scowled at her, "When I say I want a tea, I mean I want a mug of tea, not this swill." Harry Denham was not a tall man, neither was he broad, but he was wiry and he had a face which said, 'don't mess with me'.

"Please Harry, we don't have any fresh tea, it's still on ration, I have to use the leaves again, you know I do," pleaded Mary.

Harry shouted across the room, "Well, not for me you don't, you silly cow."

Young Steve, ten years old last birthday cowered in the corner of the kitchen. His dad was a fearful sight when he was mad. And he did get mad often. His dad seemed to have an air of menace about him when he was at home, but when he had seen him in the street with the neighbours he changed into this jovial 'happy go lucky' soul. People seemed to like him. "How you doing Harry?'' They would wave and shout across the street. Steve was confused but old enough to think that perhaps it was something to do with his mother. Dad always said it was, so maybe it was true.

Mary had married Harry Denham in 1937, a couple of years before World War II broke out and he seemed a nice man, a good catch, her mother said as much. But Harry went off to war like many of the men in the town and when he came back it was a different man who returned.

Mary hardly knew him. He was sullen, demanding and flew into a rage as quick as sixpence. Five years of war had changed many men, some even enjoyed their wartime experience and missed the excitement when it ended. Going back to a dull routine was very hard for them to adjust to.

But for others the horror of war changed them in a bad way, many years later it would have a name, PTSD, but for now men just had to try and get on with life. And for many like Harry, the war continued in their heads. He had his old job back again at the steel works but money was tight and rationing was still in place on lots of items.

The only saving grace was that he didn't take his temper out on the boy. Mary found that if young Stevie had done something to upset Harry, if she stepped in quick he would turn the focus of his rage onto her. She had taken a number of beatings over the last year. More than once she had to go to the shops trying to pull her headscarf down low to cover a bruised eye. The woman in the grocers always gave a her a funny sideways look. She once confided in her next door neighbour, who surely must be able to hear some of the rows going on in her house. But, she just shrugged her shoulders and said, "They're all like that dear, bloody men, they don't know they're born. They think that just because they have spent a few years in Khaki It gives them the right to knock us women about." From that Mary assumed that she had the occasion slap as well.

At the outbreak of war with Germany, Harry had joined his local infantry regiment of the Sherwood Foresters, who had traditionally recruited from the counties of Nottinghamshire and Derbyshire since 1881. Mary was distraught, she pleaded with him not to do it, "You don't have to do this Harry, you have a wife and a baby boy, let the others go to war who don't have families."

In truth Harry didn't have to enlist as he was in a protected occupation working in the steel works and, in fact, the country was going to need more and more steel over the coming years. But Harry was adamant, "I'm not having anybody call me a bloody 'conchie'." Being a 'conscientious objector ' was probably the worst thing Harry could ever imagine, they were often ostracised within their own community. Even though Harry could say that he was exempt, the risk was too great for him and many of his friends alike. Plus, there was an element of bravado and the thought of going to war with the Germans had a certain appeal, all his friends at work had joked what they would do if they got the chance. So, no amount of tears and begging from Mary had any effect, Harry joined up and went off to war.

The 2nd battalion of the Sherwood Foresters was involved in heavy fighting throughout the war years. They were part of the British Expeditionary Force which was beaten back by the Germans and had to be rescued by the flotilla of boats from the French beaches of Dunkirk.

If that wasn't bad enough they were later part of 'Operation Shingle' which landed at Anzio in north west Italy. The landing onto large tracts of reclaimed marshland went well initially, but then, because the Allied Forces didn't take advantage of their initial success, they were surrounded by the German Army and were bombarded unmercifully.

The Allied Forces lost 7,000 killed, 36,000 wounded or missing and 4,500 were captured by the Germans. Harry's war had a disastrous effect on his mind, he saw friends blown to pieces and his head was filled with desperate thoughts of kill or be killed. He was in a permanent state anxiety and fearfulness that, at any moment, his death could be in the next few seconds.

When Harry was 'demobbed' in 1945 a different Harry was sent home with a couple of medals and the heartfelt gratitude of the nation. Even though he was home and safe now, his mind was still fighting the battles in his head. He was still nervous and agitated, he couldn't sleep and was constantly on his guard against some perceived danger. He had terrible nightmares and would wake up thrashing about, scaring Mary half to death. But the worse part for him was that the slightest loud noise would send his mind right back to the marshlands of Anzio and the horrors he had experienced. To make matters even worse, working in a steelworks was not the quietest of places, but what choice did he have, he was lucky to even have a job at all.

Harry knew he was a changed man, he knew that he flew into a rage at the slightest thing, but he just couldn't help it. Mary pleaded with him to talk to her but he just brushed it off and tried to lock the memories away. But unfortunately for Harry and for Mary and for Steve, the memories kept returning and Harry just couldn't stop them. Some war veterans could process the memories and leave them where they belonged, in the past, but for those like Harry, and there were many, there was no past and no present, they were both the same.

Mary was worried though, what would all the rows do to Stevie? He seemed a delicate boy but she had noticed that he was starting to show some disturbing behaviour. He was only ten years old but had started answering her back and saying things like, "I don't have to listen to you." She would give him a clip round the ear but this only seemed to make him worse.

Then there was Mrs Anderson down the road who said that she had seen him with another boy on the recreation ground tying a firework to a cat's tail. She wasn't sure whether to believe that or not, perhaps it was the other boy's idea, surely Stevie wouldn't be so cruel. Maybe she should have a word with old Dr. Robinson about him.

Chapter Two
1957

"Steve turn that music down, I can't hear myself think." Mary Denham called up the stairs to Steve who was in his room playing records on his new Dansette record player.

Steve ignored her as usual and turned the music up even louder. 'All shook up' by Elvis Presley blared out of the stereo speakers, what had happened to real singers like Frank Sinatra Mary thought, she shook her head, if it wasn't one man giving her grief it was another. Harry had died in a factory accident when Steve was only fourteen, it was officially recorded that he slipped into the 'ladle' which contained tons of molten steel. The truth would never be known but some said that Harry fell into it intentionally.

Either way Harry's war was over. With his compensation payout and his war pension Mary had managed to scrape by. Now Steve had been working in the garage for four years and he was earning decent money. Not that she saw much of it. He spent most of it on himself, on fancy clothes, bright blue suits with velvet collars and pointy shoes.

Mary missed Harry, not the rows of course, but even with all his violent behaviour she had still loved him. She was a widow now, but then so were many women in the area and many didn't have men who came back from the war at all.

Steve came down the stairs to his mother in the kitchen, "Dinner ready yet?"

His mother looked at him. "I don't think I like your hair like that, it's very long."

Steve scowled at her, "Well its a good job then that my hair has got sod all to do with you."

"Don't speak to your mother like that Stevie."

Steve replied with a sneer, "Why not, if it wasn't for the money I bring in where would you be? I'll talk as I like."

Mary sighed, this was obviously her lot in life. "When are you going to bring that new girlfriend of yours home, I would like to meet her?"

Steve replied, "What, Susan, I'm not bringing her to this hole, Susan comes from one of those posh houses up on the Wimpey estate. She's a stunner, I'm going to marry her"

"Have you asked her? Mary said becoming interested.

Steve said with a swagger in his voice, "No, but I'm going to soon, she'll say yes. I'm sure of that."

Mary thought that it would be nice to have a daughter-in-law, somebody she could relate to, maybe go shopping with or talk about hair and make up. She sighed, thinking of weddings and grandchildren.

Steve brought her back to earth, "Daydreaming again mum, come on, get my dinner on, I'm going out in a bit".

However, Steve didn't ask Susan to marry her, at least not then. Susan was not as keen on Steve as he obviously was on her. They had been on several dates to the cinema but he appeared a little too overbearing for her. Eventually Susan said to him that she thought that they shouldn't see each other anymore, she was nineteen years old and was starting her training to be a librarian and she didn't want a serious relationship just yet.

Steve was devastated and couldn't understand why she didn't love him as much as he loved her. When he pressed her she said, "Well for one thing I am not keen on the way you dress". Steve was following one of the fashions of the late 1950's for young people, often referred to as 'Teddy Boys', bright coloured suits with long jackets, 'drainpipe' trousers, which were almost skin tight and 'winkle picker' shoes, which had long pointed toes. Steve thought he looked modern and smart. However, Susan was more conservative in her outlook. Once when her mother had seen them together she had been very disapproving, "I don't want you mixing with that sort of person," she had said to her with one of her frowns on her face.

However, Steve was not going to be put off that easily. Susan was his girlfriend and he was not going to give up. He then set out on a programme of pursuit. He worked in the garage of a large car dealer as a mechanic so he approached the manager and asked if he could move into the sales department. He was told that he would be given a trial if he smartened himself up.

So Steve bought himself a classic dark grey suit and had his hair cut in a more traditional style. He then set about a prolonged assault on Susan's defences, flowers arrived, chocolates and other small presents and he arranged to be wherever she went.

He actually did quite well in the showroom, he understood cars and could really sell the features to customers, and if wanted to, he could be very charming indeed, particularly if he thought it was to his advantage.

Eventually Susan relented and acknowledged his efforts and her friends said he must really love her to do all that. So, he wore her down and she agreed to go on dates again with him. Steve was over the moon and after a three year wait he asked her to marry him in 1960 and they were married in June 1961. Susan looked radiant and Steve looked smug and victorious.

Chapter Three
1967

The wind flew through John's hair which was fashionably long for a police constable in 1967, just about as long as he could get away with, but only just. He peddled faster down the hill towards the city centre police station, aware that he was cutting it fine … yet again. Several times he had been late for duty and the last time he had been hauled in front of the Superintendent and was given a final warning.

The trouble was that he really liked to sleep, he shouldn't have been late, it wasn't even an early shift for goodness sake, it was one forty five in the afternoon, but the residue of the previous night's drinking session was threatening to join him on his bike. He swung his old bone shaker of a bike into the yard just as one of the section sergeants was walking across, nearly knocking him for six. "You crazy bastard Cooper, watch where you're going. And you're late!"

"Not quite yet Sarge', John quipped." He threw his bike against the riverside wall running along the edge of the police station and quickly ran through the side door into the locker room grabbing his jacket and helmet on the way. Skipping quickly into the parade room just before the Sergeant he stood panting with another dozen of his colleagues.

"Get in line", shouted Sid Jones, one of the Central Section sergeants and a dozen police constables lined up in two rows across the room, already dressed in full uniform and ready to go out on foot patrol in the city. No police women of course, in 1967 they still had their own separate section, including rank structure. It would be several years yet before anything resembling equality permeated into the police force. For now it was very much a man's world with smoke filled rooms and an 'alpha male' attitude to most things.

The shift Inspector walked into the room, or rather his stomach came in first followed by the rest of him. Inspector Jim Brown or behind his back 'Tubby" Brown waddled in, how he managed to button up his jacket was a complete mystery. Sid called the officers to attention, "present accoutrements", he called and in unison they all pulled out their handcuffs in their left hand and their truncheon and whistle in their right hand.

"As you were, stand easy", he called. If you had forgotten either to pick up your truncheon or handcuffs you could just about get away with lifting up your hands with nothing in them, particularly if you were on the back row. They really didn't take much notice anyway. Tubby's eyes were on the books in front of him on the lectern and Sid was walking back to the front. This was just a ritual. In any case nobody ever blew a whistle and if you did nobody would answer it anyway and as for the truncheon, what good was a 12 inch stick of wood against anybody, all they were ever used for was knocking on doors. The handcuffs came in pretty handy though, but only on really violent prisoners.

But these traditions were a comfort in some way, John liked the idea that policeman had been doing this for the last hundred years or so and probably in this same room. Looking round it seemed the decoration hadn't changed much either. It was a dull room, all the paint in the building was brown and the walls were some sort of cream going on brown in places. The furniture was heavy and gun metal grey in colour, serviceable but not very modern. The place was kept very clean but still everywhere smelled of ancient dust and polish. There was an ambiance of no nonsense about the place, as if this is a place where work gets done, but don't expect to enjoy it!

After reading out a list of missing persons, wanted criminals, stolen vehicles and major crime over the last 24 hours Tubby handed over to Sid to allocate beats for the shift. "Cooper, area C, keep an eye out for Jimmy Haynes, we want him for those break-ins."

"Yes Sarge," replied John in a clipped voice. That would be fun, trying to arrest Jimmy on your own, it would take at least three of you to hold him down. John thought, If I do happen to see him I'll make sure I call for some help first!

The group were wheeled out in line and marched out of the station. Drill and marching was still a big thing in the police force. It had its roots in the military, even its ranks and insignia mirrored army ranks. And of course most of the older officers had been in the war and served time in one form of uniform or another so marching in double file seemed quite natural, but for John's contemporaries in their mid twenties it seemed like an unnecessary imposition. As the squad came to various points, officers peeled off in ones and two's to go to the various beats.

John stepped to one side at the end of the High Street together with Bryan East. "You look rough", Bryan stated as soon as they were alone, "On the beer were we last night?"

"I might have had a couple of pints down at the George", John replied.

"Couple, my arse, more like a dozen looking at those eyes." Bryan said, looking almost concerned but with a twinkle in his eye. He was a good few years older than John and cut a bit of a fatherly figure on the shift, men looked up to him, he wasn't ambitious and had never looked for promotion but was content to do his job and do it well.

Bryan was one of many policemen who had joined up straight after the world war two. He had over twenty years service in now and had spent a good few years in CID. The rumour had it that he had a big disagreement with a Detective Sergeant regarding the way a case was being investigated. The dispute, so the story went, was settled in the backyard. Bryan came out top but ended up back in uniform the following week.

John admitted, "Ok, well it might have been a bit of a session, but you know how it is when some of the lads get together."

"I do indeed", nodded Bryan, "but you need to take it steady, I'm not the only one who could see, Tubby noticed".

John looked doubtful, "What, Tubby, he doesn't know what day it is." he said scornfully.

"Don't you underestimate him," Bryan replied, "he may have gone a bit to seed now but in his day he was a keen 'copper'".

John shook his head and with a look of incredulity said, "Gone to seed, gone to seed, he must weigh twenty five stone, looks like he is ready for harvesting let alone seeding".

"Well, just you be careful", Bryan said as he waved goodbye and went down the next street towards his beat.

Left alone John had time to think. Maybe he had been going at it a bit much of late. He lived alone in a pokey one room 'bedsit' in the city centre, no television and just a portable radio for company. Going out in an evening with one or two of the men from the station was an easy habit to get into, if nothing else just to pass the time between shifts.

John's family all lived thirty or forty miles away and he could only get to see them when he had a couple of days off and even then it involved at least two bus journeys and took a couple of hours. John's mum and dad had been so proud when he became a policeman and travelled all the way to Harrogate to watch him 'passing out' at the training school. John had an elder sister who worked in a bank and as far as they were concerned both their children were in 'professions'.

They came from a class of person who didn't have great ambition for themselves and even a tiny step up the ladder was a big thing for them. John loved his parents, they had brought him up with kindness and with a sense of duty and personal responsibility. John thought he should really try and get to see them more often, his mum really laid the red carpet out when he visited. It was a bit of an embarrassment really and he could see his sister, Carol, roll her eyes in despair, as if to say I don't get any of this and I'm here for them every single day. Maybe he ought to get himself a motorbike, he had been threatening to for some time. He hadn't got anywhere to keep it but that was a minor matter he could solve later.

The sun was shinning and John's mood started to lift. He loved walking the beat. Of course he could drive and had passed the driving test to drive police cars but his preference was to walk. Not only did it keep him fit, it also gave him contact with people. A contact he sadly missed in his off duty time.

The City centre was a bustling place with shoppers and business premises but the outskirts were residential with parkland and river walks. John had been on the beat for eight years and now knew a good many people, if not by name certainly enough to pass the time of day. Ok, so the warmth of a police car might pull a bit during a cold winter's night shift but on a day like today there was nothing like being able to wander at will along the streets and paths he knew so well.

There were always the places where you could be guaranteed a cup of tea and a sit down. Everybody knew them, the familiar places, the night-watchmen, the hospital, the shopkeepers or the local cafe who would make you a drink and even a meal if you wanted it whilst sat in the kitchen. With it came the chat, who was doing what and to whom, which all gave a breadth of local knowledge which might one day come in handy.

But most policemen also had their own private places, 'cup of tea spots' which were known only to them and which they kept to themselves. Maybe an old lady or man whom they had visited for some reason and knew they would be always welcome back for tea and a few minutes of respite.

John made his way down one of the side streets to a house he often visited. Knocking on the door he was warmly welcomed by a woman in a flowered cotton pinafore, hair done up in a headscarf and a cigarette dangling from the corner of her mouth. "Hello Johnny boy, fancy a cuppa?"

John smiled, you couldn't help but like Nancy. There were no 'airs and graces' and if she didn't like something she would be only too quick to tell you so.

"Sure thing Nancy," John replied, "where's Pop today?" Pop was Nancy's long suffering husband, who actually thought the world of her.

Nancy replied, "Oh him, he's out with the dog but he'll be back soon."

John had first met Nancy and Pop three years before. He had been one of the officers who attended a fatal motorcycle accident. A young man had skidded on ice. The law on making helmets compulsory was not to come in for another five years. Unfortunately the boy wasn't either wearing a helmet or protective leathers when he skidded off his bike at forty miles an hour into a brick wall. They say that he died instantly, but then they always say that. John had the unpleasant task of informing his parents who were Nancy and Pop. He was their only son and they worshiped him. The news tore them apart and John made certain that he called to see them every few days for weeks afterwards just to check how they were coping. Over time they gave the outward appearance of normality but John knew they were still grieving.

John sat in the kitchen and watched Nancy pour water into a large kettle and place it on the stove. "They do have electric kettles now you know", John said with a smile.

"Oh I don't want any of that modern stuff,' Nancy said, ash dropping from the cigarette onto the floor, "it only goes wrong and you end up chucking it away, this kettle has done me fine for the last ten years and will do another ten."

John smiled they had had this conversation many times before. "What's the news on the street then Nance?"

She replied, "Not much happening really, I hear Jimmy Haynes' flogging cheap stuff down the pub and his Brenda is about to pop with their first kiddy but other that it's been pretty quiet of late."

John's ears pricked up at the mention of Jimmy. He had crossed swords with him once before and he was not a person to mess with. He was a small time villain but went in for body building and had arms and shoulders like a gorilla. John pulled out his pack of cigarettes and lit one carefully thinking if he should pursue this conversation further. One thing he didn't want to do was to get Nancy and old Pop into any trouble with the locals, nobody liked a police informant, official or otherwise.

John decided just to keep it general. "You say Brenda is about to have their baby then?"

Nancy replied , "Yep, and old Jimmy is over the moon, didn't think they would ever have a kid of their own but these things happen."

John finished his cigarette and drained the last of his mug of tea, "Well better be off, say hello to Pop, tell him to take it easy."

Nancy waved a hand, "Ok, Johnny, see you around."

John walked down the street thinking about Jimmy Haynes. Would it be worth trying to arrest him on his own? He was wanted for a number of burglaries and thefts from shops in the City. His fingerprints had matched up on several of the breaks and on the last one he had been seen and identified by the nightwatchman.

But, so far Jimmy had managed to keep one step ahead and every time the CID had been to his house and searched it he was never there. He either had a good hiding place or was being tipped off they were coming for him. No, the only way to pick up Jimmy was on the off chance. Like most famous arrests which have hardly ever been through planning, more through just plain luck, pulling up a motorist because they had a light out or bumping into someone when they were off guard.

Of course you can occasionally, make you own luck and this is sometimes where local knowledge comes in handy. John thought if Jimmy was that keen on this new baby he wouldn't be leaving Brenda for too long, or ever be too far away from her. Say what you like about Jimmy, but he was besotted with Brenda and she could do nothing wrong as far as he was concerned. Since they were married five years ago he had showered her with gifts, true most of them were stolen, but the thought was there.

So, Jimmy and Brenda's house backed onto some allotments and John knew that Jimmy's uncle kept one of them because Pop had an allotment for his vegetables only a few yards away. These were places of safe haven for many men and a growing number of women. Places where they could go, dig, weed and forget about the world, losing themselves for a time in an oasis of nature in the middle of the city. Many had little sheds on their patch, ostensibly to store garden implements, but often were like little holiday homes with an easy chair, small gas stove for brewing a cup of tea and for spending an extra hour or two contemplating the world and its problems.

Jimmy's uncle had a shed. Would it be worth just going and having a look John pondered? Maybe just to establish if Jimmy could be there and if that was where he hid out he could tell the CID and that would be a feather in his cap. He wouldn't have to do anything really would he?

John found that he had wandered towards the allotments without really giving it much more thought. He saw the shed belonging to Jimmy's uncle which appeared locked up and deserted.

Perhaps not then, but just as John was about to turn away he saw a small line of cigarette smoke drift out of the eaves of the shed. Well, well, well, thought John. So why lock a shed unless you didn't want anybody in. John stood back and just when he was considering leaving the shed door opened and out stepped Jimmy Haynes.

He stopped and stared at John and the two squared up to each other. Jimmy was a good three inches taller than John and thirty pounds heavier. He flexed his muscles under his T shirt and took a step towards John who stood his ground. "So, you reckon you can take me again do you Cooper?"

John recalled their last confrontation, on that occasion he had had the advantage of two other colleagues but he still remembered the bruises from the battering Jimmy had given all of them before he was subdued. John saw a vein on Jimmy's forehead, he watched it pulsing and knew that he was ready for a fight.

"Well", John said, "not on my own maybe, but I'm not stupid enough to come on my own. Like last time I have some backup. I just need to shout and they'll come running, Who do you have on your side?"

Jimmy eyed him up and they stood without speaking. Jimmy was the first to break the spell. "Okay, so I know I'm going down for this lot, but not yet, not until Brenda has had her kid."

John looked hard at him, "So how do you think this is going to work out then Jimmy?"

Jimmy relaxed his fists and looked John in the eye, "There are some bad coppers and some good ones but I reckon you're not one of the bad ones. Give it a day or two until Brenda has the young un and when I know she's ok I'll hand myself in."

John couldn't help himself smiling, "Jimmy Haynes handing himself in and why should I believe that?"

Jimmy replied, "Because I know I can't go on the run with Brenda and the kid and I don't want anything to stress her out. If I go down I know the family will take care of them, but I'm not doing it until I see she's ok."

John looked at him hard. What choices did he have? He didn't really have any backup so he couldn't very well take Jimmy down on his own anyway. What would be the harm in letting him go, he wouldn't leave the area that's for sure. "Let's just say for a moment that I agree, how will that work?"

Jimmy smiled knowing he had his way out. "I give you my word, that's how."

John took an instant decision and stepped to one side, "Until the baby then Jimmy," as he watched him saunter away.

Had he made the right decision, who knows? Was it cowardice or pragmatism, either way it was too late. If he had tried to arrest him he would have probably ended up amongst the peas and carrots anyway. John looked round quickly to see if anyone had witnessed the spectacle, there was just one man on the other side of the allotments bent over his plot who didn't seem to have noticed.

Chapter Four

Susan gazed out of her kitchen window looking at her garden. It was a nice garden. It was a nice house in a nice area. The Homesfield Estate were all new houses, all very neat and clean. Everything about her life was nice, - looking at it from the outside.

But Susan felt so desperate and alone, she had married Steve thinking this was what she wanted. A nice home in a nice area. Steve had been attentive before they married, thinking back, perhaps over attentive. Flowers arriving at her place of work, always making sure that he was there to meet her and take her home. But, once the newness of marriage had worn off he had become possessive and jealous of everything.

He wanted the house to be, not just tidy, but immaculate all the time and flew into a temper if anything was out of place. He re-arranged ornaments so they were exactly the same distance apart. He 'advised' her on the way she dressed, even on her make up and hair style.

If she changed anything in the first few months and years of marriage he just went into a sulk but in recent years that became an angry outburst and on more than one occasion he had struck her.

Of course, like all violent men, he was sorry the next day and brought her flowers and promised it would never happen again. If only she hadn't done, whatever minor infringement she was accused of, he wouldn't have been so angry, didn't she understand that? Susan felt trapped. She had confided in her mother but she just told her that Steve was a 'good man' and she shouldn't expect perfection.

Perfection, she didn't want perfection or anything close, in fact she would settle for anything that wasn't him. In fact a bit of mess would seem like heaven to her at the moment. She knew that her parents had just rubbed along together, she had never witnessed any real signs of affection between them and suspected that her mother thought that was enough to expect from a marriage. However, Susan wanted more than that, she didn't want to live a life never knowing what to expect from one minute to the next. She found the whole thing so tiring.

But she couldn't see a way out either. She had studied and was training to become a librarian before she met Steve but he convinced her that she didn't need to work. Steve was a car salesman and he could be very pleasant and charming to customers, so usually made quite a few sales and a good commission. People who didn't know him well would say how lucky she was to have such a pleasant man who obviously adored her. He had said at the beginning that he earned enough for the both of them and she should be happy to be kept by him and to be there waiting for his return home.

Instead she dreaded it. Until he stepped through the door she never knew what sort of mood he would be in. If the house was to his satisfaction and if everything had gone well at work the evening went usually reasonably well. But, if he had lost a sale or if he spotted something not quite to his satisfaction, the evening started to go badly from the start.

He would start by admonishing her saying, "Why do you do this, you know how angry it makes me?" If Susan apologised and promised that she would do better in future, sometimes this would settle things down, but not always.

Sometimes he would work himself up into a rage, telling her how useless she was and how grateful she should feel. If, on the rare occasion, she spoke back that's when he really would lose his temper. At first he would smash things around the house, usually things of hers and then the beatings started.

At first it was a slap which then became a punch which became a punch and a kick. Susan genuinely felt in fear for her life on occasions. But, who could she confide in, slowly her friends had all disappeared. Either she hadn't bothered keeping up with them because Steve didn't approve of them, or they had given up on her and didn't want to be associated with them as a couple when there were so many other people who were less of a problem.

She should have listened to her friend, Sally. She had said, even before they were married, "There's something not quite right about your Steve."

"What on earth do you mean?" Susan had said somewhat affronted, "he's absolutely charming."

"Yes, I know," said Sally, "but have you noticed, he never talks about anybody but himself, he never once asks anything about anybody else!"

All the warning signs were there, she just didn't notice them or if she did, chose to ignore them. She had not seen Sally in years now, probably got three kids and a dog by now.

They had a dog for a time, a puppy, Steve said it would be like a family, going for walks together, teaching it tricks and things. It lasted two days, until it made a mess on the hall carpet, then it was straight back to the breeder. Susan missed the dog, at least it had been something to talk to for a while.

A few weeks later she had seen Mrs Parker on the High Street. She was the breeder whom they had purchased the puppy. She asked Susan how the puppy was getting on? Susan replied, "But my husband brought it back several weeks ago."

"No", Mrs Parker said, "I've not had any puppies returned."

Susan asked Steve about it later that evening, "I saw Mrs Parker in the High Street, she asked after our puppy?"

"Really, how strange," said Steve. He had a very odd look on his face which Susan couldn't quite fathom.

"What did you do with it Steve?" Susan asked quietly.

 "I told you I took it back." Steve said emphatically, "Actually, thinking about it, I didn't give it to Mrs Parker it was her husband, he must have sold it on again and not told her about it." Susan didn't believe a word of it, but there was nothing she could do now to help the poor little mite.

She thought, I wonder what did happen to Sally. One day she just stopped ringing and when Susan telephoned her she was quite distant. Sally was a hairdresser and a good one. She had met her when she first came to the city and they had hit it off straight away so she wondered what went wrong, was it something she had said or done?

What Susan was completely unaware of was that a couple of years ago Steve had become completely jealous of the influence Sally had over Susan. He said, "What is it with you, it's Sally said this and Sally said that, don't you have a mind of your own. I really don't think she is a good influence on you and I would rather you didn't see her anymore".

Susan said, "Oh don't be silly, Sally is good friend, perhaps my only friend."

At this Steve became angry and said, "You don't need other people when you have me, you should know that."

A few days after that conversation Steve was waiting for Sally when she finished work. He caught up with her as she walked to her car. "Can I have a word with you Sally?"

She turned and saw it was Steve, she kept her face impassive, she had never liked Steve and she didn't like the way he spoke to Susan. Good gracious if her husband spoke to her like that he would soon get it in the ear. "Ok, but make it quick I have to get home."

Steve said, "Ok, well Susan and I have been talking and I, we, don't think that it's a good idea for you to mix together so much. Susan would tell you herself but you know how she is, I said I would talk to you in person."

Sally looked him straight in the eye, she didn't buy any of this and knew Susan pretty well and that she would never say anything like that. "Ok, well let Sue tell me herself."

Steve lips narrowed in irritation, "Her name is Susan, not Sue, and she would be too embarrassed."

Sally said, "I just don't believe you Steve." getting angry. And Sally was quite able to stand up for herself, Susan had seen her more than once deal with difficult customers in the salon.

Steve decided to take a different approach. "Susan is my wife, and what I say goes, if she really is your friend you will leave her alone. You don't want to get her into any trouble do you?"

Now Sally was really angry remembering the unexplained bruises which often appeared on

Susan,"Trouble what sort of trouble, you mean like the last time you slapped her around."

Steve's anger was rising but he felt Sally was perhaps in a different league and would not be so easily manipulated. "Just leave it, Sally, I am warning you."

"Oh warning me now, are you?" Sally said, "Well, just you listen here buster, don't you go threatening me or else you will see my Billy round to yours and then you will be sorry." Sally's husband was a big man who played rugby most weekends and the thought of him reigned Steve in.

"Well, just leave her alone is all I'm saying", Steve said quickly and with that he stormed off.

"Slimy toad," Sally said out loud.

But over the last few years Sally had kept her distance, as much for Susan as anything else. She knew that if she tried to interfere in Susan's marriage it would probably end up being the worse for her. She had talked it over with Billy and he had said, "I have known men like him before, they think they are big if they can lord it over a woman, but they are cowards really. Having said that, I think you could make it worse for her so best forget about it."

It happened to be Susan's birthday a few days after the confrontation with Steve in the street, so she just sent a card and in it she wrote, "Happy birthday Sue, just remember I am always here for you". Susan never got the card, it was thrown in the bin by Steve before she even knew it had arrived.

So Susan just carried on, day after day, week after week. Steve had wanted children, but the thought of bringing a child into this situation was something she wouldn't even consider. Steve thought something was wrong with her, of course, why she couldn't she conceive, it must be her fault! But secretly she took the 'pill' and hid them away.

Susan looked at the kitchen clock, he would be home in a few minutes and a feeling of dread washed over her. How she hated that bloody clock!

Chapter Five

Steve looked at the clock on the showroom wall, soon be time to go home. What a lousy day it had been. First that silly cow of a woman had wasted an hour of his time looking at a second hand Austin 1100 and then she walked away without buying it, even after he had turned on all the charm and given her a test drive. And then, to beat it all, the manager had announced the regional winner of the top salesman of the year award and it went to that snivelling little runt Tom Jennings at the Manchester branch.

What a stupid fiasco, couldn't they see that he was the best salesman they had ever had. Ok Jennings might bring in more money, but that was because they had the Rover dealership. But Steve sold more cars per year and it was sales that counted, right! What idiots he was working for, if only he had his own garage he would be able to show this lot a thing or two. But no, fate had declared that he had to work for prize idiots who did not appreciate his worth. He hoped Jennings would fall under a bus on his way home, serve him right!

At least it was Friday, they always had steak at home on a Friday evening and Susan cooked it with a peppercorn sauce just like they did at the Bernie

Inn. That would be some small compensation and he found himself thinking about his steak on the drive home.

He parked his Austin Allegro on the drive. It was a company car and he hated it. He couldn't understand why they couldn't have supplied him with something a bit more stylish. Anything, rather than this barrel shaped family car. Something a bit more sporty would suit his character a lot better. And the colour, it was a dried out mustard colour, even if had been bright yellow it might have been ok, or better still red, he could have lived with that. He'd tried to suggest to the sales manager that he really deserved something a bit better but it had fallen on deaf ears.

He locked the car and looked around. Everything looked in order, the grass was neatly cut, beds of flowers just starting to poke through in neat rows in the border and the idiot who lived next door had swept the leaves from his half of the drive for a change.

And Susan would have his dinner ready as usual. Susan, good old Susan, he could always rely on her to do as she was told. She appreciated him and knew what side her bread was buttered on. Ok, so sometimes he had to slap her into line a bit but that's what men did. That's what his father did and as far as he was concerned that's how all men should behave. Master in their own house and no nonsense.

And Susan was a real beauty and he knew other men looked at her when they went out and were sick with jealously because she belonged to him. He didn't mind them looking to appreciate his good fortune, so long as that's all that it was. He didn't take kindly to anyone trying to chat her up if they went for a drink, he would soon put a stop to that. He only had to give 'his look' at Susan and she would know to give any man the cold shoulder.

He walked up to his front door and into the hallway, taking off his shoes he could still see the feint stain where that little brute did his business, no amount of carpet cleaner would get it back to a pristine condition. He grinned, the little sod couldn't swim so well with a brick tied to his collar, Steve smiled at the memory, he liked to get even.

He could hear Susan in the kitchen getting dinner ready. She greeted him at the door, "Hello love, how's your day been?"

Steve said sullenly, "Lousy so far, but that can only get better, give me a kiss."

Susan kissed him on the cheek and gave a forced little smile. "Lamb chops for dinner", Susan said, in what she hoped was a cheerful voice to mask her inner tension.

"What do you mean lamb chops, where's my steak, we always have steak on a Friday?" Steve whined.

"Well, tonight I thought we would have lamb chops, the butcher was all out of steak." Susan said trying her best to placate him.

"What do you mean, why don't you order it every week?" Steve was getting irate, he had had a bad day and it was starting to develop into a really bad day. "I put up with crap all day at work, trying to earn money for us to live a good life and this is what I have to put up with. All I want is what we always have, why the hell can't you get anything right you stupid bitch."

Steve's neighbour was on his driveway and heard the row starting, he nodded to his wife, "They are at it again, the miserable bastard is giving Susan a hard time, something about steak this time."

His wife was a matronly figure who worked at the local hospital as a cleaner, she shook her head in disgust, "One of these days I'm going to call the police before he kills her".

****

"Calling P.c. 1046 Cooper, come in please", John's radio crackled. Police patrol cars had VHF radios but the issue of personal radios had only occurred that year. They were in two pieces, a receiver clipped onto the inside of the jacket lapel and a separate handset transmitter. The reception was never that great and the batteries often wouldn't last a full shift, but they were better than the old way.

Previously officers had to make points every hour either at a telephone kiosk or one of the 'silent policeman' police boxes spread around the city. Immediate response was virtually none existent. But now, not only were they always contactable, it also meant they were free to walk their beat at random.

"Go ahead, Cooper over". John replied.

"Hello John, domestic disturbance, 10 the Crescent, Homesfield Estate, neighbour just called it in. I'll get Charlie 1 to cruise round the area in case you need any backup".

"Roger that," That's all I need, thought John, a domestic dispute to round off my day. He started walking quickly through the streets to get to the Crescent. No 10, he had not had that one before, usually these were a regular thing. Go in, sort it out, try and get the wife to make a complaint, she refuses, get the husband out of the house until he calms down. At the worst get the wife and kids away to a relative. But nine times out of ten a few weeks later you would go through the same routine once again. At the same time, there was always the concern that the majority of murders were as a result of domestic arguments of one sort or another, so you never quite knew what you were walking into.

"Calling P.c. 1046 Cooper come in please", The control room came back again.

"Go ahead, Cooper over". Jon answered.

The control room gave John some more information. "According to the voters register there should be a Steven and Susan Denham living at that address. Give us a shout if you need any help".

"Thanks for that, Cooper out." John had just arrived at No 10 The Crescent, a very neat semi-detached house on the estate, Allegro saloon on the drive. Who drives an Allegro John thought, that's more of an old mans car?

He could see a woman peeking through the curtains at No 8, probably the person who rang it in.

Everything seemed quiet so far as he rang the front door bell. A man in his late twenties came to the door dressed in a two piece grey suit, white shirt and blue tie with a large silly grin on his face. He looked a bit nonplussed when he saw John on the doorstep, "Yes, what can I do for you officer?" he said in a slightly oily voice.

John said, "Good evening Sir, are you Mr Denham?"

Steve replied, "Yes, that's right, is there a problem?"

John continued, "Well, that all depends, we have had a call to say there may be some sort of trouble here."

 "No trouble officer, who said there was?" Steve said in a placating tone of voice which rankled John, like someone scratching their nails along a blackboard.

But John said calmly, "I'm afraid I can't say that Sir, is your wife at home?"

Steve said warily, "Yes, she is, why?"

John countered, "Could I come in and have a word with her."

Steve was now getting irritated and the unctuous voice being replaced by a tight lipped clipped tone. "I don't think that's convenient constable, you see my wife is taking a bath at the moment."

"Well, how about I just come in just to check everything is ok, I don't mind waiting a few minutes." John started to ease his way in without asking for much more of an invitation.

Steve was getting angry but he knew he couldn't throw his weight around with this constable. "Really officer, I don't think that is necessary, there has been some mistake, perhaps it was the television somebody has heard, we do tend to have it on rather loud."

John was actually starting to enjoy the exchange and the fact that he was putting this man under some pressure."Oh what were you watching then?"

Steve seemed a bit confused, "Well ere, Eastenders I think."

"Strange," John said looking quickly round, noticing the TV was turned off, "didn't think Eastenders was on until 7pm".

Steve was clearly flustered now. "Well, it could have been something else I wasn't taking much notice". He said very quickly and dismissively.

John didn't believe a word he was saying, he was taking an instant dislike to Mr Denham, he had met his sort before, all prim and proper up front but something seedy lurking below the surface.

He looked round, there was no sign of any disturbance. In fact the house looked like nobody actually lived in it at all, more like a show house really with everything perfectly in its place. It was a bit different to John's scruffy bedsit, but John thought even my bedsit is more homely than this place. "Well, if I can just have a word with Mrs Denham I will be able to write it off as a malicious call." John could hear some movement upstairs, in these new houses you could easily hear people moving about, and it certainly wasn't the sound of a bath running. John took off his helmet and sat on the sofa, "How about a cup of tea?"

Steve stared at him in disbelief, "What?"

"A cup of tea while we wait for Mrs Denham," John said smiling.

Steve was not used to being ordered about, not in his own home, and certainly not to make tea. But if he refused would the policeman think it strange? "Yes, well, ok then." Steve went into the kitchen and put the kettle on wondering how quickly he could get rid of this meddling policeman. And as for those nosey bastards next door, well he would sort them out somehow and get his own back for causing this embarrassment.

John sipped his tea and looked at Steve over his mug, he looked agitated. "Why don't you call your wife down now Mr Denham?"

Steve glared at him, if looks could kill John would be laying flat out dead, but he put on a grimace of a smile, which didn't fool John, and went to the bottom of the stairs and called, "Susan, darling, would you come down here a moment, there's a policeman here?" emphasising the word policeman. A couple of minutes later Susan came into the room.

Several things struck John immediately. First how attractive this woman was, long blonde hair with the most beautiful large blue eyes, there was something about her which John couldn't quite place, it was like she was someone he already knew. However, if he had ever met her before he was certain he would have remembered her. Maybe she was similar to an actress on the television or in films. Whatever it was John felt a strange and urgent need to take care of her. The second thing which was obvious was the heavy make up. It looked like she had plastered it on with a trowel and not that carefully, in fact as if done in a hurry! John had seen it all before, dark glasses, headscarves, make up covering the bruises. In fact he could still see a slight bluish tinge to her left cheek.

"Mrs Denham?" John greeted her.

"Yes, that's right, what can we help you with constable?" Susan said trying to keep her left side away from John's view.

John said, "Just checking that you are ok, we had a report of a disturbance."

Susan kept her face turned to one side. John said, "You have got all your make up on, are you going out somewhere nice, if you would like me to walk you anywhere I can do that?"

Susan replied with a little stutter. "No, no, just staying in tonight."

 "Looks like you have a bit of bruise coming there." John said in a quiet voice.

Susan's hand immediately flew to her cheek. "No, oh, well, no, it's just that, we were fooling about and

I fell into the kitchen cupboard, stupid really." She blushed and looking direct into John's eyes her hidden message was, "leave it".

John said in a quiet measured voice, "Well, ok then, so long as you are both ok. I tell you what I will just leave this card with you. It has some useful telephone numbers on it, just in case you, or even a friend say, might need them. We have to leave one of these you know, tick the box sort of thing". John's eyes never left Susan's and there was an unspoken communication between them. John knew and she knew that he knew what had transpired.

Steve stood witnessing this exchange getting more and more agitated, he really didn't like the way this constable was looking at his wife. How dare he do that? John turned to Steve and his face changed from a kindly smile to a hard stare, he looked directly at Steve this time and said, "Well now, this is my area and I will be around all evening, just in case, I'll call back again in couple of days just to follow up."

"No, you don't have to do that", Steve blurted out, "really that's not necessary."

John said, "Oh, but I'm afraid it is, it's protocol Sir, we have to do that before we can sign off the incident." This was total rubbish but Steve would never know that.

With that John gave one last knowing look at Susan, put his helmet on and walked out of the house. The neighbour was still peeking through the curtains and John resisted an urge to wave to her just in case it confirmed to Mr Denham who the complainant was.

John walked down the street and a persistent thought came to his mind. Where do I know her from? It was almost as if he had known her all his life but yet never known her. She must resemble someone he knew, but who he couldn't fathom. Perhaps it was someone he saw regularly but in a different context, perhaps like at the supermarket checkout and without that context he couldn't quite place her. But, at the same time he was sure that she was familiar. The thought bothered him throughout the rest of his shift.

Chapter Six

For the next two weeks the thought of Susan Denham kept popping up in John's mind. He couldn't figure it out, he had had girlfriends over the years, one or two which turned into semi-serious relationships but then fizzled out, usually by mutual consent. But nothing serious now for a couple of years.

He sat in his bedsit and pondered the issue. Perhaps bedsit was a bit harsh as a description but it certainly wasn't a luxury flat. It was situated in one of the old large Victorian houses just off the City centre. One large downstairs room, which would have probably been the main lounge in its heyday, now acted as bedroom, sitting room and dining area. He had a little kitchenette and a tiny room just big enough for a toilet, wash basin and the smallest of showers. All very cramped but enough to satisfy John's basic needs.

It was furnished in old second hand furniture which was part of the rental agreement. The furniture was all brown, mismatched and looked as if it had all seen better days, more than likely picked up in a sale room at auction as job lot to furnish a number of such bedsits.

But it was home, it was all he needed and was very convenient for getting to and from work, he kept his bike in the hallway and he could be down at the station within 10 minutes, as it was mostly all downhill. Not so much fun on the way home after a shift but it was getting to work on time which was John's problem.

In truth it wasn't a lot different to the home he had left. His father was a manual worker at the steel works in his home town and their rented house was furnished with pretty much a similar style and decor, so, John saw no reason to change it. It was like an old slipper really and since he never threw dinner parties he didn't really care what other people thought.

John had been to some married colleague's homes at times and a good few were on the new estates, but all they seemed to do was cut lawns, paint guttering and worry about paying the mortgage. Whilst John hoped to settle down with a family, and maybe a dog, one day he wasn't in any hurry.

Perhaps he had not met the right woman yet, which turned his thoughts yet again to Susan Denham. He must stop doing that, she was a married woman and for all he knew happily married, most of the time anyway! He had checked the records on his return to the station and there was nothing recorded against either of them. So either it was a first or, like many, gone unreported in the past.

He was starting a week of night shifts so slowly got himself ready for work, pressing trousers, polishing boots. It was a warm Spring so it should be a pleasant week of night duty. John liked night duty, you never quite knew what it would throw up. The first few hours were usually hectic with pubs turning out followed by the clubs and then the quiet time from around 3am. The time of the burglars and thieves. It could be a reasonably relaxed week or hectic and there was no way of telling and that's why he like it.

The night shift briefing parade went as usual with 'Tubby' reading out the list of stolen vehicles, wanted persons etc. "You can strike Jimmy Haynes off your list." He said, "Apparently he just came and handed himself in this afternoon, said something about a promise he had made. If it was it's the first promise a Haynes has ever kept." This was met with guffaws from the lined up officers. John stood shaking his head slightly, Well I never, he thought, he really did it, nothing can surprise me now. As the Inspector was leaving he looked over his shoulder and said, "See me in my office Cooper before you go out." What's all that about, thought John.

"Told you so!" Bryan whispered and winked as he went past.

John followed 'Tubby' into his office where he immediately sat behind his desk, his stomach keeping him from pulling his chair too close. John stood in front. There was no other chair in the room anyway so it was obvious to everybody that they must stand. The carpet in front of 'Tubby's' desk was worn thin for a couple square feet in front of the desk. John smiled every time he saw it, being reminded of that was where the phrase 'being carpeted' came from. 'Tubby' looked at him over his half rimmed glasses, "What are your plans Cooper?"

"What for Sir, tonight?" John answered.

'Tubby' said, "No, you young idiot, I mean for the future, any thoughts about CID or promotion?"

This caught John off guard, he had not actually thought about any future further than the next week. "I have not really given it a great deal of thought Sir."

'Tubby' continued, "Well, I have been keeping an eye on you for a while and I think you've got some potential. You could, if you put your mind to it, go a long way. Why aren't you married yet?"

Another question which kept John off balance. He knew that police officers who remained unmarried were suspected of being homosexual and were viewed with a degree of suspicion. Homosexuality was still illegal and would remain so until the summer of 1967. John thought, bloody cheek. But at the same time he knew most of his contemporaries were now married and many with children, so he perhaps did stand out as being something unusual.

"No Sir, still looking, not found the right girl yet, but trying hard." He tried to laugh off the insinuation.

'Tubby' said somewhat dismissively, "Well, get on with it, if you want to get on in 'the job' a steady home life helps. Anyway give it some thought and we will talk again in a few days. Carry on. Oh and cut the boozing down".

John smiled at the last remark but thought, that's a bit of a laugh, he had seen more broken marriages or at least unhappy ones with police officers than enough. Shift work and the type of work did not always sit well with regular family life and often placed a strain on it, particularly if you were a CID officer.

But John walked out of the police station feeling quite pleased with himself. At least he had been noticed and thought well enough of to consider that he was worth more than just walking the beat, much as he enjoyed it. Perhaps it was time to consider his future, time was moving on, he had signed up for thirty years but he was getting close to already having completed a third of that time.

Tonight he had one of the City centre beats and the first few hours went as normal. As usual for the first few hours he tended to stay fairly close to the main areas around the Market Place where most of the city pubs and clubs were and which caused the majority of trouble. There were a few drunks and a bit of rowdyism but nothing out of the ordinary. John went into the station at 2am for his 'refreshment' break of forty five minutes.

The police canteen provided meals twenty four hours a day. They were usually very unhealthy meals of 'fry ups' or chips with anything. Occasionally though there were some left over food from the lunch time where a decent meal was offered for the daytime office staff. Mostly though police officers either brought sandwiches or relied on the fatty fair being offered.

John was no exception, he ordered a plate of egg and chips. John was a bit lazy when it came to cooking at home plus he didn't exactly have a great kitchen. So most days he would just eat a meal at work during his shift and this gave him the ability to just snack at home with something on toast or a sandwich. John had not much finesse when it came to food and had been used to plain cooking when he was a child. After he had finished his meal cooked up by the night chef he went back out to his beat and began patrolling the back alleys and shops.

Finding people sleeping out in shop doorways was not an unusual thing and in fact the city centre had its regulars well known to all the police, usually well soaked in cheap wine or sherry. They were sad characters really and usually had a story behind them of broken marriages, alcoholism and despair. John knew them all and usually kept an eye on them during the night, keeping away any hooligans who thought it fun to throw bottles at them or worse.

Every so often they would cause enough disturbance to get arrested and taken into the police station where they were de-loused, given a bath, some better clothes from the Salvation Army and put in front of the Magistrates the next morning. They were then given a fine, which they never paid, usually followed by a couple of weeks in prison where they dried out to a small degree and then back on the streets again. It was a sad existence which lasted until either the cold or the alcohol claimed them. These were the hardened ones, not the occasional or temporary rough sleepers, if they had been given a home they would go straight back onto the streets.

John noticed a bundle of clothing in the doorway of a shoe shop whose entrance went round a corner and created a little space popular with homeless men and sometimes women. He shone his torch just to see who it was and his light lit up the face of Susan Denham. It was debatable who was more shocked Susan or John.

"What on earth are you doing in here?" John asked incredulously. But as he looked more closely he saw the left eye slightly closed and already blackening.

"I've left him this time, just walked out this evening. I really don't have anywhere to go and no money to get me there even if I had."

"Have you tried the women's refuge on Curzon Street," John asked.

Susan shook her head and said in despair, "I tried there but they can't take me until Thursday, they suggested I try the Salvation Army. So I thought I would just sit here and wait until morning and try them later on".

John was trying to think fast, this was a situation he had not come across before, a rough sleeper whom he felt personally responsible for. "What about family and friends?" He asked.

"No, that's not good", replied Susan, if I went to my parents they would just send me right back home, they just don't understand, or perhaps don't want to understand. As for friends, well, I don't have any close friends any longer, not that I could just land on in the middle of the night, Steve saw to all that and drove them all away. Anyway, he would look for me there and I am scared next time he will really hurt me."

John made a quick decision, "Well you can't stay here all night, goodness knows what might happen to you. I could no more leave you here than fly to the moon."

He saw Susan give a slight smile. John said somewhat hesitatingly, not sure how his suggestion would be taken, "Look my place is close to here, I am on night duty so nobody is there, you are welcome to spend the night there and in the morning we can see if we can sort something out."

She looked almost deflated with relief, "That's so kind of you, I can't tell you what that means to me, I'm not really the roughing it type."

John smiled, "No, I gathered that from your home, don't expect the same with my place though, I'm just a bachelor and it's a small place. Look take my key, the address is 22 Leonard Villas, it's on the ground floor, go through the front door with this key and it's on your right. Let yourself in and help yourself to anything, not that there is much there."

Susan stood and looked at the key in her hand, "You're my guardian angel, bless you Pc Cooper."

He replied. "Better call me John if you going to sleep in my bed!" They both laughed at this. "Look I will be in about 6.30am so try and get some sleep until then".

John watched her walk away and wondered if he had done the right thing. It was obviously the wrong thing as far as his job was concerned. He should not get personally involved. But there was no way in the world he could have seen her sleeping on the streets. What else could he have done with her under the circumstances other than leave her there in the doorway.

Suddenly anger burned up from his stomach at the thought of Steven Denham beating her like that. He didn't ask what had started the argument, it didn't matter. Come what may he would protect her from the bully of a husband.

The rest of the night John walked his beat and thought about Susan sleeping in his bed. It gave him some contradictory feelings. One of pure joy that she was close to him and one of sheer anxiety at what he may have set in motion. At 6am the shift were dismissed and John put his anorak on and started the slow ride up the hill to his bedsit. He had a spare key hidden in the garden of the house because he was always locking himself out with the Yale locks when the door blew shut, so he had no problem entering quietly.

Susan was curled up fully clothed on top of his bed with a rug pulled over her, her blond hair spread out on the pillow. John stood for a moment and just looked at her and a feeling of pure happiness spread over him that she was here. He tip toed over to one of his two easy chairs and sank into the broken seat. He removed his boots and decided to get a few hours sleep before waking her.

The next think John knew he was being gently shaken. Susan was bent down in front of him. "Hey, I thought you were going to wake me when you came in, it's 11 am." John stared at her for a second until his brain came into gear and the events of the previous night came back to him.

"Well, in that case we better have some breakfast."

They sat opposite each other at John's small table eating scrambled eggs and toast. "I told you my flat wasn't much."

Susan smiled, "At the moment to me it is like heaven. I haven't felt as relaxed in years."

"What will you do?" John asked.

Susan thought for a moment, "I'm not going back to him, if I did things would be ten time worse, I know that, but I do need a plan and I'm afraid I haven't got one. Just really did all this on the spur of the moment."

"Most people do," John replied, "they reach a tipping point and just get out. Look I know it's not much here but I am on night duty all this week and so you welcome to stay here. I can assure you that you will be perfectly safe."

"I don't doubt it for a minute." Susan smiled mischievously. "You are very kind, if I can get out and pick up a few basic things I can manage until I get myself together. I hate to ask you this but could you loan me some money, I walked out, or rather ran out with nothing."

Of course, I can," John said, "I don't have much cash on me but enough for you to pick up the basics, I'll go to the bank later and draw out some more for you."

Susan relied, "Thank you John, you don't know what this means to me. By the way, have we met before? I have this strange feeling that we know each other from somewhere".

John agreed, "I know, odd isn't it, I get the same feeling but no idea where that could have been."

Susan took the few pounds that John gave her and went out to the local shops to pick up a toothbrush, comb and some basic makeup. She also picked up a few bits to make some lunch. It occurred to her that, it didn't matter what she bought for them to eat that it would be just fine with John. The thought struck her like a hammer blow, how much she had been controlled by Steve in her every thought and action and how quickly she was now feeling a freedom from it. John's 'bedsit' was a bit rough and ready but actually it felt more comfortable than her fancy new house had ever been.

Chapter Seven

Steve Denham was pacing up and down his lounge, he had been awake all night. When Susan walked out he had shouted after her, "And good riddance, see how long you can cope without me." He expected her to come crawling back within the hour. So he went to bed determined that if she did try and come home he would ignore the doorbell until she was good and cold. At which time he would let her in and she would be repentant. That would be good, he liked it when she was sorry. It gave him a feeling of power that he never normally felt.

So he lay in bed and after several hours he started to worry. Where was she, she didn't have any friends in the city? Her parents were miles away and she didn't take her handbag when she went out. The longer it went on his mood went from an anticipation of victory through concern to anger. The bitch was doing this just to spite him. He rang into work the next day feigning illness and said that he needed a couple of days off to recover from a really bad cold. Of course they accepted his excuse, nobody wanted to see a sniffling, coughing salesman. So Steve sat and brooded and the hours limped into several days.

****

Meanwhile, John and Susan seemed to have set up a little working arrangement of bed sharing. She slept at night and when John came in after his night shift they swapped over and she either sat and read from his small library of books or went for short walks into the nearby park. When John awoke they sat and chatted, toasting muffins on the two bar electric fire and enjoyed telling each other their life stories so far. But as much as they talked they couldn't still figure out where their paths had crossed before. What they both felt though was, this felt right, they seemed to fit together, hand and glove, yin and yang.

It was bound to happen at some point and they both felt it. They were sitting side by side on the single bed when they just looked at each other and both knew what was going to happen next. They fell into each others arms kissing gently at first and then more passionately. The following day instead of waking John with a cup of coffee after his turn in the bed Susan slipped in under the covers with him. John awoke to find her naked body next to his. They made love, gently and with great tenderness. John was aware of the type of behaviour she had experienced in her marriage and was determined to show that not all men were brutes.

For the next couple of days they loved each other and it was almost as if they had their own little home together. John was stunned how easily he found being with Susan, they seemed to share the same ideas on just about everything. They laughed at the same things, they enjoyed the same books, the same films, he couldn't find anything that he did not like about her. The whole thing was uncanny.

Likewise Susan was shocked that she had walked out of a very unhappy and violent marriage and straight into another relationship with a man. That certainly had not been her intention. When she walked out on Steve it was not supposed to be straight into another man's arms. However, with John she just felt like she belonged there and one of the most amazing things was that there was no tension in the air, something which she had become used to on a daily basis. Without that ever present atmosphere of dread she felt she could at last be herself and she was loving it.

Back on the Homesfield estate Steve was getting desperate. How could she leave him, she knew that she needed him to take care of her, to explain how things should be and what to do. She would be lost without him, and nobody could love her as much as he did, didn't he show that all the time?

Where could she be, he had made tentative enquires with her parents and unless they were better liars than he gave them credit for they had not seen her or been in contact. Susan's mother had said, "What's wrong Steve, why are you asking, don't you know where Susan is?" Steve just made up some excuse that she had gone out that morning but he wan't sure where she was and was just checking up to make sure she was ok.

If Susan's mother disbelieved him she chose not to say anything, either to him or Susan's father. He rang several of her old friends, some were definitely cool towards him particularly that Sally bitch who said straight out, "Has she finally left you then?"

"No, of course not," Steve replied.

"Yeah well right, if she has, good is all I can say," Sally said as she slammed the phone down.

He thought she may have gone to Sally's but after sitting outside their house for almost 24 hours non stop there was no sign of her.

What else could there be? It suddenly occurred to him that copper took more than a passing interest in her. He remembered him giving her a card, Steve thought, I bet the pig had put his own telephone number on it. He couldn't remember his name but if he sat in the cafe opposite the police station at shift change overs he would be able to see him and perhaps follow him. He felt pleased with his plan, at least he was doing something. If Susan thought that she could make a fool out of him she would be sorry when he found her.

The same evening Steve sat in the little cafe opposite the police station and made a cup of coffee last whilst he watched and waited. Sure enough there was the same policeman going into the police station on Sunday evening at 9.45pm. He was a good looking man, tall, broad shouldered with dark hair and a face that a lot of women would go for.

Steve felt instantly jealous, the thought of this man even touching his Susan made his blood boil. An intense hatred for the man boiled up inside him. If he was starting at 10pm that would mean that he would be off duty at 6am thought Steve. Right an early start then for him for the following day.

At 6am on Monday morning Steve was again watching the police station, parked up in his car across the road and down a small side street.

John cycled out of the police station a few minutes later and Steve started to follow him at a distance. It was easy, not like trying to follow somebody in a car, he just had to keep well back and he could keep his eye on John from a distance. Steve resisted the temptation to surge forward in the car and knock him of his bike. He fought hard to control the urge, otherwise he would never know where he lived.

When John turned into Leonard Street he watched him go into No 22. Surely Susan couldn't be in that dump of a place, he was starting to have some doubts now. Susan wouldn't be in any place like that. Steve considered going up and knocking on the door. What would he say though, is my wife here? That would make him look like an idiot, he wouldn't do that, better to watch and wait.

****

Sunday night duty at the police station was always followed by a quick change over to an afternoon shift on the Monday. This ensured that the next two days which followed were rest days and would be complete days off. John had talked to Susan about it and they had decided they would try and get away for those two days and spend them in a hotel somewhere, perhaps in the Peak District.

They had sat and planned it together, John would hire a car and they would drive out into the Peak and they would try and put the City and Susan's problems behind, even if for a few days. They were both excited about the prospect of being together like a real couple. The very idea seemed like heaven to both of them.

John managed to get a few hours sleep before he was back on duty again at 2pm. Quick change round from nights to an afternoon shift was always bad and threw your body clock completely out of sync. But he was allocated a beat in the centre of the city and at least he didn't have any traffic duty points to cover.

Susan on the other hand felt wonderful. She felt light headed and had never been so happy. So she thought she would rather like a new skirt and a top if they were going to go away for a couple of days. She barely had any clothes other than a few bits and pieces she had picked up just to get her by throughout the week.

Susan decided that she would go into the main shopping area of the city and buy herself something that would please John on their trip. He had given her quite a bit of cash so her choices would be quite wide. She was rather looking forward to this. To be able to buy something just because she liked it, what a lovely change that would be. It could take a couple of hours but she had nothing to do until John finished his shift at 10pm.

She walked quickly out of the house and down the road to the city centre. She didn't notice the Austin Allegro parked at the top of the road. As soon as she came out of the house Steve saw her and got out of the car and started to follow her on foot at a safe distance that wouldn't draw her attention.

He had spent the last six hours trying to come up with a plan of action. His mind swung from pure hatred and violence through to self pity. Eventually his plan was to suddenly meet her in the street, as if by accident. He felt so sure that once she saw him again she would relent and fall into his arms and beg him to take her back. He knew that she couldn't possibly be happy living in that dump of a house. Susan liked things ordered and just so, like he did.

He was convinced his plan would work, why wouldn't it, she needed him. Susan drifted into a few shops but was so intent on her purchases she didn't notice Steve approach her.

****

"Calling P.c. 1046 Cooper come in please", John's radio crackled.

John answered, "Go ahead, Cooper over".

The control room came back with the message, "Hello John, looks like there's a disturbance on the High Street between a man and a woman, can you make your way please."

John thought, it couldn't be, could it? A feeling of dread flooded through John's body and he ran to the High Street. There was a crowd of people and in the middle he could see Steve Denham dragging Susan by her hair along the ground. John's mind seemed to go into overdrive, thoughts flooded his brain, that was Susan, the woman he loved, he ran into the crowd drawing his truncheon. "Leave her alone you bastard," he shouted.

He swung his truncheon at Steve with the intention to hit him across the arm he was dragging Susan with. On the few occasions that Steve had been taught self defence and arrest techniques at training school he was always taught to hit on the primary targets which are large nerve clusters. Those were the common peroneal nerve in the mid-thigh and large, easily targetable muscle groups, such as the quadriceps and biceps, but never the head.

Steve saw the blow coming and instinctively ducked to avoid it, but the blow landed squarely on his temple. Steve fell like a sack of potatoes onto the pavement. People in the crowd gasped. "That was a bit much," someone said.

John bent over Susan, "Are you alright, has he hurt you?"

"Nothing I won't get over", Susan sobbed.

A man in the crowd said, "I think you need to have a look at this feller".

"What do you mean?" John said turning and looking at Steve lying on the ground. He went over and looked down at him. He was very still, too still, he couldn't see his chest moving. "Stand back", Steve shouted and felt for a pulse, …nothing. "Control from Pc. Cooper",

They answered, "Go ahead John".

"Ambulance to the High Street, emergency, man not breathing", John said breathlessly.

Control said, "Did you say man?"

"Yes, man", shouted John. He tried to give Steve CPR, pumping on his chest, interspersed with mouth to mouth resuscitation.

"Stand back, stand back", came another authoritative voice, it was Pc Bryan East from the adjoining beat. "What's going on John?"

John said quickly, "I meant to hit his arm Bryan, but caught him on the side of the head, he's not breathing."

Bryan looked at his friend and said, "You did, bloody hell?"

The ambulance arrived and Steve was lifted in. The door closed and it sped off to the Royal Infirmary blue light flashing and bells ringing.

Chapter eight

John was sat in the interview room at the police station. On the way in he had poured out the story to Bryan. "Bloody hell, bloody hell", was all Bryan kept repeating.

The door of the interview room opened and Bryan came in with a mug of hot tea. He sat close to John and spoke in a very quiet voice, "Now you listen to me son, and listen hard to what I've got to say, because I have only got time to say this once. That character Denham is dead."

John looked at him in horror, although he already feared the worst from what he had seen. Bryan continued, "Now all that business with his missus, you forget it, it never happened, Ok? I've already had a word with his wife before she's interviewed and put her in the picture."

"What do you mean, why shouldn't I tell them," John said in a whisper.

Bryan said in exasperation, "Because, you idiot, you are in enough trouble already, they are going to say that you used excessive force on him."

"But he was dragging her with her hair Bryan." John looked at his friend for support.

Bryan replied, "Yes, I know but he didn't have a knife to her throat did he, she wasn't in immediate danger of death was she? And you killed him in front of half the bloody city."

"I didn't mean to," pleaded John.

Bryan patted him on his shoulder, "That's right and that's the story you stick to. From what she tells me he was a bad bastard. But if they find you have been screwing his missus all week they will charge you with murder. Do you get it now through your thick skull."

John looked confused, "But lots of people must have seen her coming and going from my place".

Bryan said, "Take my advice son, admit to anything short of murder and they won't go looking for witness', believe me John you are in deep shit, your job is over, you just need to come out smelling as sweet as you can from this. Now I have to go, I only came in to give you this tea. I'm not supposed to talk to you, a Federation Rep and a solicitor are on their way. Remember what I said. You're a good man and a good copper John, so best of luck mate."

"I didn't mean to kill him Bryan, he ducked and that was it." John said quietly.

Bryan put his hand on John's shoulder shook his head and said, "I know lad, I know, some men can be shot or beaten half to death and they come up smiling but others, one bang on the head and they're a goner."

John said, "That's all it was Bryan."

Bryan looked at him sitting slumped in his chair, nothing like his friend of a few hours ago. He looked broken. "Listen, the word is that they are sending a couple of senior detectives down from HQ because you are a serving police officer."

"Who are they Bryan?" John asked.

Bryan answered, "One is a Detective Superintendent Bailey and the other, I think, is Andy Jones a Detective Inspector."

John looked at the desk shaking his head in confusion, "I don't know those, do you know anything about them Bryan."

Bryan said, "Well, Jones is a 'good un', Bailey can be a bit of an arse, I served with him when I was in CID but Andy Jones should keep him on the straight

and narrow. Now I better get out of here." With that
Bryan left the room leaving John stunned and
confused. It would take some time to process all
this, meanwhile he thought it best if he said very
little and tried to keep Susan out of it.

****

Susan sat in an adjoining interview room still trying
to absorb what that other policeman had said. Was
this a trick? No, it couldn't be, it did make some
sense to her. Oh how happy the last week had been
and now what a dreadful mess it had all turned out
to be and the man she had grown to love in such a
short period of time was going to be in such serious
trouble. But she must protect John now. If that
means saying nothing about their brief affair then
that's what she must do. Surely it would all get
sorted out then they could be together? Perhaps
they could move away somewhere? Anywhere
except this dreadful city with so many awful
memories.

****

John was interviewed some four hours later, a
Detective Superintendent Bailey and Detective
Inspector Jones came from Headquarters especially
for the job. John was cautioned and told he was not

under arrest. You understand what that means said the Superintendent?

John replied, "Yes of course, I've given the caution hundreds of times".

"Don't get smart with me sonny boy," the Superintendent barked.

So that's how it's going to be thought John, no friends here then. Bailey continued, "According to records you attended the Denham household some three weeks ago to a domestic dispute, what happened then?"

"Nothing happened' replied John, "all quiet on arrival, as they say, the husband had obviously knocked her about but she wouldn't make a complaint."

Bailey asked, "So have you seen either of them since that date?"

John paused for a fraction of a second, "No, I don't think so."

"Don't think so, or no?" Bailey came back quickly.

"No," said John more emphatically in a voice which he hoped came across as believable.

Bailey continued with the interview, "We have witness statements from two people in the High Street this afternoon which say that you went launching in like a madman and hit Mr Denham over the head."

John looked at his solicitor for some indication of how he should answer. He just appeared bored looking at his nails, some use he was going to be John thought, I wonder where the Federation dug him up from.

John answered, "No, that's not what happened, I was trying to save Mrs Denham and I tried to strike the upper arm to connect with the nerve to make him drop her."

Bailey sneered, "Oh very clever, where did you learn that one."

"It's standard practice now sir." John said more calmly than he felt.

Bailey said, "Is it, well why didn't you just ask him to stop?"

John knew he was now getting into difficult territory, "Well, er, because I believed Mrs Denham was in grave danger of being seriously injured."

Bailey leaned back in his chair, his eyebrows raised, "Really, was she? By pulling on her hair, in what world is that a danger to life?"

John was struggling here and he was starting to know it. Would it be better to say nothing? But then they would think he had something to hide, best try and be open. "Well, he could have had a weapon."

"Did you see any weapon?" Bailey asked.

John answered, "Well no, but he could have had it secreted on his person somewhere". John had been present at enough interviews to know he was sinking. Telling lies did not come naturally to him. Now he knew what many offenders who had sat in front of him must have thought, 'tell the truth and go down, or try and lie your way out of it'.

Detective Inspector Jones produced a police truncheon in a plastic evidence bag. "This is the truncheon taken from you this afternoon, do you recognise it?"

John looked at it, "Yes that looks like mine".

Jones said, "This is much heavier than a standard truncheon, can you explain why you are in possession of it?"

John looked confused, he had not expected this, "No, you see this is a standard truncheon, it's just an old fashioned one. When an old constable was retiring we did a swop and he handed in mine. I kept his. It must be getting on for at least forty years old."

Det. Insp. Jones weighed the truncheon in his hand, "It seems heavy, is there a lead core or something?"

"No, you don't understand," explained John, "this is made of Lignum Vitae, it's the heaviest, hardest wood there is."

Jones said, "Lignum Vitae eh, never heard of that one, but not a standard item now is it?"

John felt almost defeated and in a quiet voice he said, "I couldn't see a problem with it, that police constable had carried it for thirty years before he gave it to me".

Bailey looked at him with a hard stare, "Well it certainly did some damage today didn't it Constable Cooper?"

The interview continued for another hour with John maintaining his innocence and that it was all just an accident that Denham had died. Just one of those things that can happen. At the end John felt wrung out.

Detective Superintendent Bailey said, "You can take it that you are suspended from duty at this point, hand me your warrant card. You will be bailed to appear back at the police station in two weeks when a decision will have been made as to how to proceed. Meanwhile you are not to have any contact with any other police officer or witness including Mrs Denham, is that clear."

"Absolutely,' replied John, with a great deal of resignation. His world was falling down around his ears. Earlier in the day he had been floating on cloud nine and now it was all snatched away, leaving him in total despair.

Chapter nine

John made the journey to his home town a few miles from the city to stay with his parents for a while. The thought of staying in the city and possibly bumping into any of his old colleagues was more than he could bear. He felt bereft, how had it all gone so wrong and so quickly.

With a great deal of regret he accepted that his career in the police was now over. If he managed to get away without being charged with a criminal offence he was certainly going to be charged with an internal disciplinary offence which would result in his dismissal. John had spent eight years with the police and loved it. It was all he ever wanted to do, even as a boy growing up. What would he do now, how would he cope if he ended up in prison? That was a thought that terrified him.

As usual his family welcomed him back. His mum and dad did not have a telephone, the same as many people in 1967. But his sister Carol and his brother-in-law, Henry, did, so he had rung them and in a long, and very much a one sided, telephone conversation had outlined his problems. His sister was older by five years and had always looked out for John as he was growing up. She was just old enough to not be in competition with him but young enough to still be close and be able to help him in so many ways. Now was no exception.

On arrival at his old home the whole family had come together and they listened to John as he sat in the front room of his parent's council house. This was the room they 'kept for best', just for visitors and not for everyday use. The very fact that they were even in there denoted the importance of this meeting. It had his parent's best three-piece suite which they had bought on 'hire purchase' over many years. It also had a new 'G Plan' teak sideboard with his mum's wine decanters standing on the side, which had actually never seen any wine. His mum kept the room pristine for the rare occasion when someone important came to visit. Someone important to his mum was the Vicar or perhaps her sister-in-law, John's Aunt Mary who looked down her nose on everybody with no reasonable cause.

John started out talking about how he had first met the Denham family, describing everything in detail. John's dad shook his head, "The bastard, what sort of man needs to beat up a woman, a coward that's what."

"Shush dad," his mum said, "let John finish".

John couldn't lie to his parents, it was the way he had been brought up, always to be honest, always to treat people as you would like them to treat you. It was a Christian upbringing and John had been encouraged to attend Sunday school each week. So when it came to the part where John had found Susan hiding in a shop doorway he told the story in full, including how he had fallen in love with her over the following week. His mum began to cry and Carol passed the box of tissues she had been holding to herself.

"Denham?" John's dad said musingly. "I used to work with a chap in the foundry called Denham, Harry Denham, any relation?"

"I really don't know Dad," said John.

"Yeh, old Harry, I was in the army with him, never quite recovered, he's dead now, some people say he did it himself." John's dad had a far away look in his eyes for a while and then seemed to snap himself out of it. "So what's going to happen now boy?"

John's dad cut to the quick as usual.

"Well", and John paused for a long while, choosing his words carefully, he didn't want to alarm them but at the same time needed to prepare them for the worst if it happened. "If they find out Susan was with me all week they could interpret it wrongly and make a case for murder. They might say that I wanted him dead, even for just that moment.

Or, leaving Susan out of it, they could find that I used excessive force that was unreasonable and that I could have foreseen the likely consequences and be charged with manslaughter. Or, I might get away with a lesser charge. In any event it's not going to be good.

But, I will plead guilty and try and keep Susan out of it."

"But why lad, why, surely if you tell the truth they will understand?" John's dad was shaking his head, he liked to see things in a very simplistic way.

John said, "No dad, you don't get it, they won't, a good barrister will twist it and a jury will see it as somebody killing his lover's husband. No, I have to keep Susan out of it, so guilty is what it will have to be to anything less than a murder charge."

Ever the pragmatist Carol said, "So how can we help John?"

"Well, one way is something both you and Henry can do for me." Carol and her husband worked in a bank, which as far as John was concerned meant that they understood everything to do with money and investments. "I have saved a bit of money over the years, not much, but a few thousand pounds. I didn't have a fancy house or mortgage to worry about so it just built up really. At some time I'm going to need money to start up again. I want you to take the money and invest it for me in some way. You two know about these things, just put it somewhere which will keep it safe and earn a bit for me."

Carol felt relieved that at least this was something Henry and her could do for him. "We can do that John, no problem, anything else."

"Just pray for me." John said with a great deal of sadness and resignation.

Carol took him to one side a little later on. "I hope she's worth it John." John looked grey from so much worry, but he tried to smile for Carol's sake.

"You know me Carol. I wouldn't settle for a woman who wasn't just right for me." John said in a very sad and dejected way.

 "No, I get that," said Carol, "your track record with girlfriends has not been great so far. But broth' she was a married woman and now you are going to be in all sorts of trouble. I just hope it's the real thing for you both."

John held his sister in his arms, thinking this might be one of the last times he would be able to do this for some while. "I don't know what it was Sis' I have never felt like this for any woman. I suppose I can honestly say that until now I didn't know what real love was."

Carol by now was sobbing she had held it in for so long, now the tears just flooded out and they held onto each other for quite a while.

****

John answered his bail two weeks later and stood in the charge office next to the cell block. This place which was so familiar to him had now became so alien. He wished the ground would just swallow him up. At this moment John couldn't think of anything worse happening to him. The shame was overbearing. Other officers seemed to be 'very busy' and were avoiding looking at him. He wasn't sure if they were just embarrassed, concerned or were being outright hostile, it was difficult to tell.

Detective Inspector Jones had come down again from Headquarters for the procedure. John was formally charged with manslaughter and bailed to appear at the City Magistrates Court the next week for committal to the next Court of Assize. "Is there anything you want to say in answer to the charge?" Jones asked.

John replied, "No, just that I'm sorry and I will plead guilty." And with that, John's fate was sealed. He walked out of the police station for the very last time, he kept his head down, not knowing what was being said about him, but caring a very great deal.

Chapter ten

Susan left the police station on that Monday evening of her husband's death in a complete daze. So much had happened in such a short period of time. So much to take in. And what that policeman had told her, she had listened of course and didn't want to get John into any trouble, but none of it made any sense to her. Why couldn't she just say she had left Steve and that he had found her and attacked her and that John had come to her rescue. What was so wrong in that? Murder, surely they could never think that. But, the policeman, what did he say his name was, Bryan? He said she must never tell anybody. And Steve was now dead. A police woman had come into the interview room and sat next to her. She had held her hand and said in a very quiet voice that her husband had been taken to the hospital but had been found to be dead on arrival.

She made her way home, why not, it was still her home after all. On reaching the house, the news had obviously spread quickly. There was a bunch of flowers on her front step. Susan just stood and looked at them, why would anybody do that? Her emotions were in turmoil, she hadn't loved Steve for a long time, perhaps never really. But she had to admit to herself that she had fallen head over heels in love with John. It had been so easy, so comfortable, so right. And now all this. At the same time she hadn't wished Steve any harm, certainly not his death. She had just hoped he would get on with his life without her. Of course underneath she knew that was too much to hope for. Steve thought of her as a possession which he was not about to give up. She had to admit that he would never have given up the pursuit of her until at least one of them was dead.

She unlocked the front door and walked into her home, no, not her home, this was Steve's home, nothing about it cried out that it belonged to her. She went into the lounge and scattered all the cushions around the floor, she brushed the pictures and ornaments off the mantlepiece with her hand and left them where they lay on the floor. She went into the kitchen and turned out the cutlery drawer and then pushed everything back jumbled up together. Then she sat in the middle of the kitchen floor and sobbed. She thought that it would make her feel better but it didn't, her life was miserable. She felt so alone.

Slowly she got to her feet and dragged herself up to the bedroom she had shared with Steve, so much misery had occurred in that room. She pulled the bedcovers from the bed and took them into the spare bedroom and lay on the little single bed. It reminded her of John's single bed and how they had had to squeeze together to prevent them from falling out. How they had laughed. She smiled to herself at the memory. Could they ever return to it? She resolved that whatever it took she would. Exhaustion overtook her eventually and she fell into a fitful sleep.

The following morning she was awakened by an insistent knocking on the front door. What now? Then everything from the previous twenty four hours flooded back to her conscious brain. It could be something to do with John, so she got out of bed still clothed from the night before and went to the door. She could see from the outline in the door glass that a woman was outside. Oh no, she thought I do hope it's not mother. Opening the door she was met with her old friend Sally. "God, you look like shit ", Sally said.

Susan tried her best to smile,"Well thanks for that, actually I feel like I look."

Sally said, "Oh, you poor darling, I am so sorry, Steve was a real prick but I guess nobody deserves to be killed. Come on I'll put the coffee on and you can tell Aunty Sal' all about it."

An hour later Sally had the full story in between bouts of sobbing and more cups of coffee. "What will you do now?" asked Sally.

Susan replied, "Well, one thing's for sure I'm going to sell this bloody place, it has too many bad memories."

Sally agreed, "Too true girl, but what then?"

Susan said, "Well, I need to see what happens with John, maybe, if he just gets probation or something, we can make a new start somewhere else."

"Hang on there Sue." Sally said with a frown across her face, "You know that can't happen, right? Not for a long time. For one thing you said he may go to prison and not only that you have to keep your distance."

"I suppose so," replied Susan, "but the thought of doing nothing just kills me".

Ever the practical person Sally said, "We are not going to do nothing, I'll come round when the children are at school and we will sort things out together." Sally promised her as she got up to leave, "Better go, the children will be home from school soon, at least you don't have that problem."

Various people came to her front door during the next few days, Susan ignored them all including her next door neighbour who seems to be holding some sort of casserole dish in her hand. When she had gone Susan opened the door and found that she had cooked a meal for her. It was very kind of her particularly as she knew how awful Steve had been towards them over the years.

Then one knock at the door came she couldn't ignore. Stood on the doorstep was both her mother and father. She let them in and after a perfunctory hug they all sat in the lounge and faced each other. Susan's father looked uncomfortable, as if he had been dragged there under protest. Her mother started the conversation, "Now dear, you know how so terribly sorry all the family are to hear about Steve's death, and in such an awful way. Your father and I were never that keen on Steve in the beginning but you couldn't say that he had not provided you with a beautiful home and we know that he worshipped you."

Susan could stand it no longer, "Mother," she almost shouted at the top of her voice, "just stop. Steve was bully and a brute who beat me black and blue. You have no idea what my life has been like, either that or you just don't care. So don't come here now telling me you are sorry, you could have helped me before, but you chose to ignore the times when I tried to tell you what it was like."

Her mother sat back as if she had been assaulted, her father looked anywhere but not at either of them. There was silence for what seemed like a long time but probably only for a minute. Her mother seemed to compose herself and said, "I realise that you are upset at the present Susan, but I'm sure things were not as bad as you are saying now, you are just grieving."

Susan thought this is hopeless they will never understand or will never want to in her mother's case. She stood up, "Mother I think you should go, I would prefer to be left alone."

Her father jumped up as if released by a spring and looked relieved, her mother stood up slowly, "Well Susan, if that's what you want, you always were a strong willed girl, we'll talk in a day or to when you feel better. Please let us know the funeral arrangements." With that her parents left and Susan slammed the door behind them.

It wasn't that she didn't care for her parents, she did. Her childhood had been fine really. But she knew that her mother liked to hide her head in the sand like an ostrich and could never cope with anything which was unpleasant. Confrontation was an anathema to her, so both her and her father had almost run their lives on parallel lines, never arguing but really never talking about anything important either.

She had even seen her mother put her hands over her ears and heard her saying so many times to her father when he mentioned something in the news, "George, I don't want to hear it." Susan thought she would have to go and see them in a week or so and patch it up. Her mother would forgive her outburst because she wouldn't want the unpleasantness of any continuing disagreement.

However, Sally was as good as her word, each week day for the next few weeks she came round and they sat and drank coffee and made plans. "First things, first," said Sally, "money, do you have any?"

Susan looked a bit nonplussed, "I suppose, there must be money in the bank, Steve dealt with all that."

"I bet he did," said Sally sarcastically. "Ok what about life insurance policies?"

Susan replied, "I have absolutely no idea Sally, but anyway it seems wrong to profit from Steve's death."

"Now, listen here young lady," Sally said putting on her motherly voice, but in truth she was only two years older that Susan. "You are going to need funds and where they came from, so long as it's legal shouldn't concern you. You are also going to need to earn a living. You are a trained librarian what about looking for a job like that?"

"Actually, I'm not trained, I never finished my training, Steve didn't want me to." Susan said thinking back to the rows they had about her working.

"Then finish it, plan No 1," said Sally with a great deal of emphasis. "Next thing let's get this house on the market in the next few months whilst the weather is fine, these houses sell well in the summer."

"Then of course," said Sally very carefully and treading softly, "there is the funeral to arrange as soon as they release the body."

Susan looked confused, "Release the body? Oh yes, of course Steve, yes I will have to arrange something".

Sally said in a very business like way, "Don't worry I'll help you."

"Thanks Sally you're being an absolute gem."

"Forget it, I feel as if I abandoned you before." Sally said. She then went on to tell her about the confrontation she had had with Steve and the reason she had kept away.

Susan said, "Oh Sally, if only I had known, I have missed you so much." They both hugged and cried on each other shoulders.

****

Susan had already broken the news to Steve's mother the day after his death. She now had to tell her about the funeral arrangements when they were completed. Luckily she got on very well with Steve's mum and she arrived early at the house on the day of the funeral. "I thought you would want someone to hold your hand dear," she said on her arrival.

Susan replied, "Thank you Mary, you are so kind, my friend Sally will be here as well of course, so we can all go in the car together".

Mary was now in her late 50's but looked 20 years older. She had moved into a small, third floor council flat overlooking the river. Steve visited every now and again but very rarely invited her to his own home, just perhaps at Christmas, but then only for a few hours. After that length of time Steve would start getting agitated, as if she were spoiling something and he would eventually say, "Come on mum, let's get you home, don't want you being out too late." What he really meant was, let's get rid of you.

Mary sat on the settee and seemed very nervous, "I'm so sorry Susan".

"What do you mean, what have you got to be sorry for." Susan looked confused.

Mary continued, speaking slowly and picking her words carefully, "I know Steve could be difficult, he always was as a child and I know that he was worse when he got older." Susan said nothing just looked at Mary, who was sitting staring at the handkerchief in her hands which she was continually winding round and round her fingers. "When you got married, I thought you would be good for him and I thought he really loved you, but I wasn't sure".

Susan sighed and felt sorry for Mary, she had heard some stories about her life. Steve had occasionally mentioned his father's temper and intimated it had been directed at Mary.

Susan said, "Things became very difficult Mary, let's just say that he wasn't easy to live with". There seemed to be an empathy between them both as they looked at each other.

Mary said in a very sad voice, "I know, I know and I'm sorry, he took after his father I'm afraid."

Susan said emphatically, "Well, it's over now Mary, let's leave it in the past where it belongs."

Mary said trying to brighten her voice but not really achieving it, "Yes dear, of course, as much as you can that is. I hope things work out for you Susan".

At that opportune time Sally arrived and a few minutes later so did the funeral car. The service was very short and held at the local crematorium, a few people were there from Steve's workplace, a couple of his cousins and a few people she didn't know, one at least looked like a police officer. There was no wake and under the circumstances everybody understood.

Sally went back to the house with Susan. Sally said, rubbing her hands together as if brushing off some imaginary piece of dirt. "Well glad that's all over, we can be sure he's gone now".

And so, bit by bit, Sally helped Susan arrange her life and things started to calm down a little, until the date of the trial arrived.

Chapter eleven

The courts of Assize were an ancient tradition which preceded Crown Courts. Circuit Judges would arrive in a town or city, a service would be held first at the cathedral. Then with great pomp a parade of officials, including the Lord Mayor, would make their way to the Assize courts for the opening ceremony. The courts were in session for a week or so in which time both serious civil and criminal cases were heard.

John answered to his bail on the morning of his hearing. He was dressed in his best blue suit with a smart white shirt and a conservative tie. He was taken into the cell area below the courts where he waited patiently for his turn.

Police officers were always assigned duty to the Assizes and stood guard in best uniform and snow white gloves in front of the court doors, jury room, corridors etc, but the duty which always caused much merriment was the assignment to the Judge's back passage.

Bryan had managed to wangle duty at the court and as John sat with his head in his hands in the austere cell, the door opened and in walked Bryan. "Good to see you mate," he opened with.

John looked up surprised but glad to see his friend, "What on earth are you doing here Bryan?"

Bryan gave a laugh, "I'm here all week on duty, white gloves and all. I haven't got long but I just wanted to wish you luck, the lads at the station are behind you. Not all perhaps, but most of them. They don't know the full story but they believe you never intended to do any serious harm to that Denham character."

John looked relieved at the news, "Well, that's good to know at least. Who is the judge in number one court?"

Bryan looked at his list, "It's Judge Lawrence."

John shook his head, "Great, that's all I need, 'black cap Lawrence', as if I didn't have enough problems." Judge Lawrence had earned the nickname 'black cap' back in the days when hanging was still a punishment for capital offences and his preference for giving the death sentence. A prison warden came through the door, "What are you doing in here?" he snapped at Brian,

"Get lost mate." Bryan snarled back at him as he walked out.

John was ushered up the steps which brought him into the dock of Court Number 1. The court rooms were in an old building built at least a century before. The courtroom itself was panelled in dark oak and the judge's bench sat high above the court room with a tall backed seat, almost like a throne, giving him a very impressive stance above the proceedings. The dock had a high wooden panel all the way around it with small iron spikes set into the top of the panels. John was a tall man but the panels still came up to his chest. Of course it was designed not only as a security issue but also to intimidate the prisoners and it was working as far as John was concerned. He couldn't have felt worse if he had tried.

The court room was full of people, barristers, news people and just ordinary members of the public. He looked around hoping to catch sight of Susan but he couldn't see her anywhere. He supposed she had already been advised he was pleading guilty and that it would not be necessary for her to attend. Perhaps it was for the best.

He recognised one or two police officers in plain clothes obviously come to watch the spectacle. He could also see his sister Carol in the gallery, he had asked specifically that his parents should not be there. He didn't want his mother and father to see him like this. The Clerk read out the charge and said, "How do you plead?"

"Guilty", was the single word that John uttered.

The prosecution barrister stood and described the brief circumstances of the incident. There was no need to go into too much detail as John had pleaded guilty. This was just a formality to get to sentencing as quickly as possible.

John's barrister stood, "M'lord if I may," he then went on to describe John's previous good character, lack of any previous convictions or misdemeanours. He read out his senior officer's appraisals of him which were all glowing. He described the incident and suggested that it was more accidental than intentional and begged for leniency,

"Very well." The Judge looked down at John from his bench. "I am taking into account your admitted remorse for this incident, I am also taking into account that you have pleaded guilty, thus taking responsibility for your action. However," and then he paused. Here it comes thought John. "I must also take into account that you were a serving police officer, a position that must be highly regarded and one which must display the highest standards of tolerance, patience, good conduct and professionalism. You acted in a manner in which you should have perceived the outcome, or possible outcome, that excessive force could cause the death of another person. As such I feel I must make an example of you. You will go to prison for a period of 10 years. Take him down".

John sat in the holding cell his head in his hands, Ten years, he'd thought a maximum of five, but ten how would he ever stand it.

At the end of the day's proceedings John was bundled into a prison van along with four other prisoners and taken to a prison some thirty miles away. John sat handcuffed in the back of the van as it bumped along. He looked at his fellow passengers. They were a mixed bunch of criminals going down for robbery and burglary. John even recognised one of them who kept giving him sideways glances.

John fought hard not to feel superior. These were going to be his equals from now on. He was a convicted felon and there was nothing he could ever do about that. He watched roads and fields fly by through the van windows. How long would it be before he saw green fields again.

A huge sadness like a lead weight descended on John, as if the last few weeks had suddenly all come together to press down on him. He fought hard not to go into a depression, if he was going to survive it would take all his reserves. He looked round the other prisoners in the van and thought, 'I'm one of them now and that's it'.

The prison was an old Victorian building but looked more ancient in its structure with its high stone walls and enormous double wooden gates. It looked more like a castle than a prison. Each prisoner was taken to the reception area one at a time where they were booked in. "Name?" snapped a prison warder with a slashed peak on his cap so that it want straight down his forehead, more like the Gestapo than a prison officer.

"John Cooper," he replied.

"From now on it is John Cooper, Sir, got it?" Snapped the prison officer.

"Yes", said John.

"Yes what?" The guard stared hard at him.

"Yes Sir", said John resignedly.

"Do you know your sentence?" the guard asked.

 "Ten years, Sir", said John.

"That's right and ten years you'll do if you don't behave yourself." The guard said in a somewhat mocking manner.

He was given a pile of prison clothes consisting of heavy serge trousers, thick light blue shirt and a short waist length jacket, a toothbrush, a bar of soap and a small towel. "In there and get changed, look sharp, you're not at home now."

John changed into the rough prison clothes and carefully folded his suit, it would be a long time before he would see those clothes again.

The prisoners once booked in were taken to their cells which were arranged in long corridors on two levels. There was a recreation area in the middle but above it was metal netting to ensure prisoners didn't jump, or 'fall', from the upper landing down to the ground.

John was led to the cell he was to share with another prisoner. The door was unlocked and he was pushed in. The door clanged shut behind him with a finality which John felt through to his core.

There was an older man laying on the bottom of two bunks. The cell contained a small wash basin and toilet in the corner, a small table and two chairs. The toilet had no seat, just a porcelain bowl, and the table had a broken leg so it tilted slightly to one side. A few personal items were on a shelf above the table, presumably belonging to his 'cellmate'.

The man on the bottom bunk looked over the top of the book he was reading and peered over his glasses at John. "Yours is the top bunk."

"I guessed as much," said John. The man went back to his reading. John climbed onto the bunk and lay on his back. If I am going to survive this, John thought I have to get into a frame of mind. I can't keep thinking about the past, what might have been or the unfairness of it all. He had read before that men who went to prison thinking they were innocent, whether they were or not, drove themselves mad.

So, it must be a matter of acceptance. Take everything as it comes and live each day one at a time. He was still young so he would get out in time and when that happened he would try and be in a position to get back on his feet again. John lay there and wondered how well this plan would work in reality!

John slept, but very fitfully, the sheets and blankets were rough on his skin, the mattress was lumpy and his dreams were interspersed with nightmare images.

At 6.30am a loud bell rang, his 'cellmate' said, "Come on, roll call". John slipped out of bed and the door to his cell was opened. A warder with a clipboard stood in the doorway, "Names?" "Ben Wood, 4312/67 Sir".

"Name?"

"Er, John Cooper, Sir,"

"Number?"

"Er, I don't know, Sir."

"New here are we, well you are 6435/67 from now on remember it." With that the door was closed.

"What now?" John asked.

"You really are new to this aren't you?" his cellmate said chuckling.

"Yes, unfortunately, it's my first time."

Ben said, not unkindly, "Ok, well now it's ablutions time, I'm going first because I have been here longer, and then it's down for breakfast followed by a couple of hours, recreation."

"Thanks, I'm John, by the way."

Ben smiled, the first one John had seen for some while, "I got that already."

There was a line of men for breakfast which Ben and John joined. When they got to the food hatches, 'trustees', that is trusted prisoners who worked in the kitchens, slopped some indescribable things onto a tin plate. John sat down at a long table next to Ben, who grinned and said, "It's not that great but you get used to it."

After breakfast they went to the recreation area. This comprised of a few table tennis tables, some cards, dominoes and jigsaws. "No snooker," Ben chuckled, "too bloody dangerous."

John found a seat in the corner and wondered what to do next. He knew that prisons were like small communities and formed of different groups. But, if you were a newcomer you would be a target just because you were different. A bit like when blackbirds mob an albino one just because it was not like them. And everybody else seemed to be in small groups.

Then a large man walked over to him, he had a
shaved head and tattoos all over his arms. "What do
we have here then?" John tried to ignore him,
"You're that copper aren't you." At the word
'copper' noise stopped and men turned to look at
them.

John thought it best not to answer. There are few
things worse than a police officer ending up in
prison, a convicted pedophile or maybe a judge, but
a police officer was not far behind. Tattoo man
snarled, "I hate fucking coppers." He hovered above
John cracking his knuckles and was slowly joined
by two other men.

A voice said, "If there's going to be any ruckus I just
want you to know I'm with him." The men turned
and there stood Jimmy Haynes.

"You're with the copper?" Tattoo man said in
disbelief.

"Ex-copper, I believe," said Jimmy, "and yes, he's
with me and I say he's ok."

Tattoo man put his hands on his hips and stared at
Jimmy, "Why Jimmy, for fuck's sake?"

Jimmy on the other hand looked almost amused.
"Because, I owe him and there are good and bad

coppers and he's one of the good 'uns. Plus what he did any man worth their salt would have done. I hate fucking wife beaters."

Tattoo man and his mates stood and stared at Jimmy, who stood a good few inches taller than all of them and his muscles flexed. The seconds passed, then Tattoo man visibly relaxed, "Ok, if you vouch for him Jimmy, that's ok with me."

John realised he had not breathed for the last minute. He let out a long breath. "Thanks Jimmy."

Jimmy smiled, "How you doing Cooper?"

John said in as calm a voice as he could muster, "Well, much better for seeing you obviously, how's Brenda and your daughter wasn't it?"

Jimmy beamed, "They're just great, thanks. Brenda comes up most weeks. Well, see you around Coop', keep your powder dry." With that he walked off to join a game of cards.

The other men kept giving John angry glares but kept their distance.

Ben sidled up. "That was a close one, but a friend of Jimmy Haynes carries a lot of weight in here, you're lucky." Lucky! John thought, that's not quite how I would put it but, one day at a time, one day at a time.

Chapter twelve

A couple of months went past and John slowly settled into the routine of prison life. With the protection of Jimmy Haynes most prisoners left him alone. There was still the odd one who spit into his food in the food queue or tripped him up in the hallways. But generally it was small time stuff and nothing that John couldn't handle.

John bumped into 'tattoo man' a few times more and on one occasion he gave John a swift punch in the kidneys as he walked past. Jimmy asked him a few times if he was being left alone and John always thought it prudent to say that he was and that everything was fine.

Carol visited several times and promised that she would keep on doing so. One day he was told, "Cooper, you have a visitor." John thought Carol must be here again, but when he walked into the visitors room he stopped dead in his tracks.

There sat at one of the tables was Susan, his heart missed a beat and his breath came in short bursts. He walked slowly over to her. No touching or hugging was allowed so he sat opposite her.

She looked at him and quietly said, "Hello John." She was silently crying and John's heart melted.

"Hello Susan, you shouldn't really be here."

"I know, I know, but I just had to see you to tell you personally a few things."

John put his hand up, "Susan, before anything else, I need to say to you how sorry I am I have brought this on. You know I didn't mean to kill Steve. I just wanted him to let go of the woman I love."

Susan smiled through her tears, "The woman you love?"

John tried to smile but found that he couldn't quite manage it, "Yes, you must know that."

Susan said, "Well that's one of the things I need to tell you. I love you too." They both sat looking into each others face. Tears streamed down Susan's cheeks.

"Now I need to tell you something else which is going to be really hard," John said slowly, "I don't want to see you again. I want you to get on with your life. If I thought that you are out there waiting for me, then every day will seem like a lifetime. I just can't tick off every hour of every day for ten years.

But if I can think of you getting on with your life, being happy then I can find a way of coping.”

Susan was sobbing now so much so that a warder came over and asked if she was alright. “Yes, yes, I’m fine, thank you.” Susan dabbed her eyes, “You sound like my friend Sally, she has been telling me similar things. In fact I have sold the house and I’m going to move away from the city. I can’t stand to be there anymore with so many terrible memories, but also so very few beautiful ones of the week we had together.”

“Good”, said John, “Move away, a long way away, try and live your life. I will always love you Susan, always, goodbye.” At that he stood and turned quickly away from her so that she couldn’t see the tears rolling down his cheeks as he walked away.

Susan never visited again.

****

Months flowed into years and one day John said to his cellmate, “What job did you do on the outside Ben?”

Ben replied, “Me, I was an artist, a portrait artist,” he said with a chuckle.

117

"An artist Ben? What did you do bump off your model?" John said laughing.

"No nothing like that," said Ben, "I used to draw the Queen."

John looked a bit confused, "What, you mean Queen Elizabeth?"

Ben smiled, "The very same, only thing was I used to draw her on bank notes." They both curled up laughing.

John asked, "Will you teach me to draw?"

Ben shrugged his shoulders, "Why not, what else I have got to do all day."

Ben turned out to be quite a character, self taught but a brilliant artist and John learned everything he could from him using any old scraps of paper they could lay their hands on.

John's lessons carried on over several months until one day Ben said, "You know if you want to learn to draw properly we will need some better materials than just scraps of paper and an old pencil stub. Maybe if you ask the warden your sister could have some sent to us. It's no good me asking, otherwise with my background they will think I'm producing 'get out jail free cards' with the warden's signature on".

"Now that would be worthwhile," John said laughing. "I'll give it a go". Ben wrote out a list including heavyweight sketching paper, a series of pencils of various hardness from 4H to 9B, a pencil sharpener, some erasers and a mortar and pestle."

"What's the mortar and pestle for Ben?"

"That's one of the secrets, if you want really fine shading you need graphite dust. So we will grind up some pencil 'lead' which is just graphite and clay. Traditionally the mortar and pestle are made of a hardwood called lignum vitae but probably she will only be able to get a ceramic one."

John looked thoughtful, remembering his police interview. "Lignum vitae eh, well there's a thing."

"It means 'wood of life' in Latin you know," said Ben.

John gave a sardonic half laugh. "'Wood of life', well how ironic is that."

Much to Ben and John's surprise a prison officer popped his head into their cell a few days later and said, "Warden says you can have those things, anything to keep you out of mischief."

So, John's art instruction went from strength to strength until one day Ben said, "I'm out of here next week."

John looked shocked, he had grown quite accustomed to old Ben, if not a little fond. "What, what do you mean?" said John with some surprise,

"I'm due for release, I've done my time," said Ben

"I'm going to miss you Ben." John said. In a different world he would have given him a man hug.

Ben laughed, "Aye lad I'll miss you too, didn't think I would when they told me that a convicted copper was going to share my cell, but you've turned out not to be that bad after all." Ben gave his usual chuckle.

****

In 1972 John had another surprise visitor. He walked into the visitors room and immediately recognised his old colleague Bryan East sat at a table. John was somewhat shocked to see him.

"Bryan, good to see you, what on earth are you doing here?"

Bryan smiled, "Just thought I would check see how you were getting on?"

"Took your time then?" John quipped.

Bryan said, "Had to wait until I was retired John, you know that."

"So you have left 'the job' then?" John stated.

Bryan replied, "Yes, 6 months ago, given them the twenty five I signed up for." They chatted for a while talking about all the people they had worked with, laughing at some of the antics Bryan described.

John went serious all of a sudden, "I did the right thing didn't I Bryan?"

Bryan became serious, "You absolutely did old son. You know I met Andy Jones a few months ago in the George Inn, you remember the DI who interviewed you?"

"How could I forget," said John.

Bryan continued, "Well, he's retired as well now. We had a few pints together and we got talking about you. Apparently Bailey was all for charging murder but Andy argued against it. The other thing he let slip was that he had found out about you and Denham's wife, Andy was a good detective. But, he kept it to himself. You were going to plead to manslaughter and that was good enough for him. The other thing which came out slowly after the trial and after you had gone down was what a bastard Denham was to his wife. Just bits and pieces came out from neighbours and so on. So, no real loss John, no real loss."

They sat quiet for a long time. "What are you doing now Bryan?"

Bryan smiled and tried to lighten the mood, "Got myself a nice little number as a porter up at the City Hospital, Peggy says I am in my element." Peggy was Bryan's long suffering wife but John also knew that she worshiped the ground he walked on.

When Bryan had left John thought long and hard about their conversation. He wasn't sure whether he should feel relieved or not. It seemed such a long time ago now.

With Ben gone, John felt a real sadness and loss. He had become quite fond of the old man over the years they had been together. He'd put up with his snoring and bad habits, but he had also learned a great deal from him. Not only how to draw but more importantly how to survive in the jungle that was prison.

How just to keep your head down and stay below the radar, not to upset anybody not to challenge anyone and to try and be as invisible as possible. Let the ones who wanted to try and run the show fight it out amongst themselves. It was a lesson which had served them both well. Jimmy had been released some while ago but it seemed as if his protection still counted and for the most part John was left alone.

But it wasn't going to be for long, John was also on the move. He received papers to say he was being transferred to an 'open prison' at Standford Hill on the Isle of Sheppey, on account of his good behaviour. So it had worked for that as well.

At first John was against the move, mainly because it meant that it would be almost impossible for Carol to visit him more than a couple of times per year. But it was the only choice offered to him and on reflection he thought any move to new surroundings would be good.

On Carol's next visit he told her the news. She was obviously glad he was going to be sent to an institution which was more targeted at rehabilitation than the dreary place he was in. Naturally she was disappointed at its location. But as always Carol said, "Look on the bright side, it's in the south so it will be a good bit warmer!" Carol also had some good news for John. They had invested his money in property, very wisely as it turned out. In the early 1970's there was a property boom and the value of his portfolio had quadrupled at the very least.

Chapter thirteen

The house on the Homesfield Estate had sold quickly and Susan was so glad to see the back of it. She got rid of much of the furniture to a local dealer. She didn't want hardly anything from the house, just a few personal possessions and the odd item. Even her clothes she threw onto the local tip along with all Steve's suits, shirts and ties. It gave her great satisfaction to sling them into the council skip. As she was throwing his golf clubs in a man came running up and said, "Hey, they look ok, can I have them?"

"Sure take anything you want, I don't care," said Sally finally glad to be shut of anything to do with Steve Denham.

Susan moved in with Sally for a few months whilst she decided her future. After her visit to John she had slipped into a depression and being with Sally's upbeat family was a tonic. Sally's husband Billy was always jovial and the atmosphere in Sally's house couldn't have been more different to her own with Steve. Gradually she started to relax. She kept looking for work and one day Sally said, "What about this one?" holding up a national newspaper.

<u>Assistant Librarian Wanted</u>

The Beaney Library, Canterbury
Must have some experiences in working in a well ordered, medium sized library and be familiar with the Dewey Decimal Classification system. Rates of pay commensurate with experience and qualifications.

"What on earth is a Dewey whatsit when it's at home then?" Sally said in her usual light hearted way.

Susan said, "Oh, that's just the system of indexing they use in most libraries, that's not a problem, I know all that. But Canterbury, that's miles away, I won't know anybody."

Sally replied, "No, and that's just the point, young lady, remember what John said to you. Get away as far as possible. Of course I'll miss seeing you but it's not a million miles away and we can always visit."

Susan applied for the job and to her surprise got an interview. She caught the train to St Pancras and then a local train to Canterbury. It was the first time she had been to this city and was impressed as she walked down the pedestrianised High Street. It had quite a cosmopolitan feel to it with street cafes and lots of foreign tourists drawn to the cathedral in the centre.

The library was on the High Street and she made her way to the librarian's office a few minutes before her interview time.

The head librarian was a middle aged woman with her hair tied up in a tight bun. She gave an impression of being 'bird like' with small jerky movements, but she seemed friendly enough. "Why Canterbury Mrs Denham?" Miss Taylor the librarian asked.

Susan answered, "I needed a change, my husband died as a result of an accident last year and I wanted a new start".

Miss Taylor looked at her application form and CV, "I see, do you have family?"

Susan thought, what a strange question and what's that got to do with anything, but she replied, "I don't have any children if that's what your asking. I have sold my house so have nothing to stop me moving anywhere, I have no ties". As Susan said this her thoughts went straight to John, saying she had no ties felt so disloyal.

Miss Taylor said, "I have looked at your resume and note that although you have experience of working in a library you have not worked for five years, any reason?"

Sure, loads of reasons, Susan thought, but none I'm willing to discuss here, but instead she said, "My husband didn't like me working."

Miss Taylor's eyes went up, "But now you want to return?"

Susan said, "I do Miss Taylor, I love books and I like people, so the two go well together."

Miss Taylor smiled for the first time since Susan had entered the room. "You are the last candidate, so I can let you know this evening, how can I contact you."

Susan stood, "I am staying at the County Hotel." She held out her hand to shake but Miss Taylor seemed hesitant, as if personal contact was something she was unused to.

Miss Taylor called later that evening to offer Susan the job. She was absolutely ecstatic, more than she thought she would be. After all, she had only been offered a job as an assistant librarian, a job she was doing anyway before she was married. But, somehow, this meant independence and a way back to the life she should have had.

Susan decided not even to go back north but moved straight away into a local Bed and Breakfast hotel whilst she looked for a permanent home. First she hired a car, she had a driving licence but had not driven for six years since her marriage to Steve. He didn't like her driving, said it worried him that she might get into an accident and in any case why did she need to when he could drive them.

Really all he wanted was to control everything she did and driving would have given her the independence he hated. So she was a bit hesitant at first but soon got the hang of it again, she had hired an Austin 1100, the gearstick was a bit sloppy but the size of the car suited her. The car hire firm had offered her an Allegro but she quickly declined.

Susan toured the city until she believed she had its layout. Canterbury was not really a very big city but there were some beautiful areas and the city itself was so full of history. She thought to herself that this was a place that she could see herself living.

She went around the local estate agents and asked for details of houses in her price range. Although she had sold her house the cost of similar houses in the south east were quite a bit higher. But she had obtained a good price for the old house and the insurance policy had paid off the mortgage, so she was a cash buyer which seemed to carry a lot of weight with the estate agents. When they showed her new houses she quickly said, "No, nothing like that, just show me older properties, in fact the older the better."

Eventually Susan settled on a small Georgian terraced house within walking distance of the city centre and the library. It had two bedrooms and a bathroom on the first floor and another small attic room. A lounge/dining room straight off the front door and a small kitchen which had obviously been added some years ago.

The previous owner had been an architect so although the house was old it had been modernised in a style which suited its age. She loved it as soon as she stepped through the door and that was before she even saw the small walled courtyard garden at the rear.

She started work at the library a few weeks later and moved into her own home two months after that. Susan furnished it with second hand furniture. Steve would have hated it. She had her own job, her own house, her own life but she did not have the man she loved, so it seemed an empty success.

Chapter fourteen
1977

1977 and John was released from prison having served his full ten years. For the last five he had served it in a category D prison which afforded him much more freedom. He had his own room, they had television, snooker and he had a choice of work related rehabilitation. He could have chosen between horticulture, workshop or catering.

John thought long and hard about how he would use his skills on his release. Who would want an ex-con working for them, possibly not in your garden or your workshop but he figured nobody cared who cooked your food, they were invisible. So he went to the kitchens but this time he learned real cooking, the idea being that he would be reasonably qualified to enter the catering profession on his release.

And he could go outside, he saw green fields for the first time in five years. So the last few years of his sentence had been bearable if not enjoyable to some extent.

Carol and her husband met him outside the prison. They hugged for a long time. "Well, little brother you are your own man now, any plans?" They went to a local hotel and stayed the night. They told John that he was now the owner of five small houses and that he had a tidy sum in the bank. Carol had invested his money wisely and as the property market boomed she re-invested it in more houses which were now being rented out giving a steady income stream.

Other money she had invested in stocks and shares in the booming IT industries which had done even better. "I don't know how I can ever thank you Carol, this will be the biggest boost to me that I could ever imagine."

Carol smiled, "Well it wasn't just me of course it was Henry as well, and actually we invested in the same things when we saw how your money was growing, so we have done pretty well ourselves. What do you want to do with the houses?"

John thought for a while and then asked them to sell three and keep two to rent. He put forward an idea that had blossomed over the last twelve months. He said, "I have been pretty well trained as a chef so I thought, rather than trying to find someone to employ me I would open up my own restaurant." He had seen one advertised in the local papers in Faversham just off the Market Place which looked promising. Carol and Henry thought that it was a great idea and became quite excited at the prospect.

So the three of them went to examine the property the next day. It was a small restaurant with a bar and 12 tables with a total seating of around fifty people. It looked like it needed updating and had closed because the previous owner just couldn't make it pay.

Before John put an offer in he decided to do a bit of local research. There were two other small restaurants in the town which were both doing well. On enquiries John found the previous owner of his restaurant was surly and the food plain and uninteresting.

John and Carol did the calculations and figured the business could work if the menu was right and the premises were updated. They estimated there was enough local and tourist trade to support another restaurant. Faversham was an ancient town which used to be a seaport but long ago the estuary had silted up. However, it was still only a few miles from the coast and whilst not a 'seaside town' like Margate and Ramsgate it would still get tourists along with regular trade.

Meanwhile Henry had been doing some research of his own. When he met up with Carol and John he seemed quite excited. "I have a bit of interesting information. The restaurant which we are thinking of purchasing and is currently called 'The Hop House', which is actually quite relevant given the historical brewing tradition of the area and Faversham in particular, also has a longer history." He paused for effect.

"Come on then Henry don't keep us in suspense spill the beans," said Carol pushing him into a chair in a little cafe where they had met up again.

"Well", said Henry, the building is very old and it used to house the Faversham gaol or bridewell, where I suppose the local drunks would get locked up for the night. So, if you buy it John, you will own your own prison effectively."

They all rolled about laughing. "Well, I reckon I could get it a bit more comfortable than the last one." John said.

"That does it then, it's an omen. If we go for this one let's call it the 'Gaol House'." No said Carol, "Lets call it 'The Jailhouse', more American, gives it a bit more style I think and more appeal."

So John decided to give it a go and the 'Jailhouse' was born. "Why do you want to stay around here anyway John? Why not come home?"

"I like the air here," John joked, "no, seriously, there are too many unhappy memories back there and also people who knew me as I was before prison. I want to make a new start. I have been scanning the local papers for the last year. I think this is as good a place as any."

John looked at them both across the other side of the table. "You two have done so much for me. So I would like you to come into partnership with me in the restaurant. I don't want you to put any money in. I wouldn't have anything if it were not for you. But I also need you because I will not be able to get a liquor licence with my conviction, so it would have to be in either Henry or Carol's name. We definitely need to be able to sell wine and beer with meals."

"Oh, we definitely do", said Henry, "a restaurant without wine is like a pub without beer."

John decided that the restaurant also needed a themed look. 'The Jailhouse' was formed and opened six months later. The place was furnished with cell like booths, decor around the place included ball and chains, handcuffs and a set of stocks at one end of the bar. The menu although fairly traditional all had a penal ring to them such as:-

Alcatraz burger

Steak with a Wormwood Scrub Sauce
Chateau d'If roast dinner
Devil's Island Cheesecake
Lockdown Chicken Pie
Diesel /tea
Kanga/coffee

He hoped the customers would get into the spirit of it as being something just a little bit different. He hired a couple of waitress', bar staff and kitchen help. Much to their amusement he furnished them uniforms with convict black arrows on. Nobody asked why he was using this theme they just thought it was all fun.

Because he was the boss he didn't have to talk about his background, everybody just assumed that the idea was a novel way of getting trade. And it wasn't uncommon, themed pubs and restaurants were all the rage in London and some of the bigger cities. There was even one restaurant where you were supposed to eat in the dark. People loved it, anything that was different.

The Jailhouse Restaurant had a 'grand opening', or more realistically it opened with a few curious customers and with Carol, Henry and John's parents, who had come down especially for the occasion. John was proud of his achievement, but not as much as his Dad. "John I have to hand it to you lad, I thought that being in prison would be the end of you, instead you have come out a better man I think and your mum and me are glad you are our son". That was very high praise from his father who very rarely said anything even remotely emotional, his mother cried a little at his speech.

The first night in the restaurant went well, people were a little bemused at the names of dishes but seemed to take it all in good spirit and the sound of laughter and chatter coming from the tables was like music to John's ear.

John lived in a small one bedroom flat above the restaurant, not much different to his old 'bedsit'. He had become so used to living in a small place that if he had moved even into a tiny house it would have felt like a barn to him.

John was doing well, but accustoming himself back into the real world was going to be a slow business. He had arranged for his parents to stay at a local hotel and by 10pm they were tired and had had enough and John arranged for a taxi to take them back to their hotel.

Carol and Henry stayed to the bitter end and after the restaurant had closed they sat with some of the staff and opened a few bottles of wine to celebrate. "I need to talk to you about mum and dad," John said to Carol. "Neither of them are getting any younger and Dad will soon retire from the steel works, I want to put them into one of the houses that we have rented out."

"They won't do it John," said Carol, "they have been in that council house virtually all their married life, to them it is home and they have all their friends around them."

"Ok then, what if we arranged for them to buy their council house and I paid for it?" John said.

"Well, you have thought this through, haven't you." Carol said smiling at her brother.

John laughed, "Let's face it I have had plenty of time to think this through Carol, - more than enough time."

Carol replied, "Well, I'm not sure they will accept it, you know how proud Dad is but we can try. We will have to sell one of the other houses to do it, but that shouldn't be too much of a problem, one of our tenants is due to move out fairly soon."

John slapped the table with the palm of his hand. "Let's try and do it then Carol, Mum and Dad never lost faith in me and I want to do something for them.

As for you two, I don't know how I will ever repay you if I live to be a hundred."

Carol just laughed, "You're my little brother and I love you, just behave yourself from now on and that's payment enough, besides you gave us the idea of investment and we have done pretty well ourselves. Remember we can get really good interest rates by working in a bank!" "Let's all drink to that then shall we?" They all raised their glasses to a new and hopeful future.

****

Over the next year the restaurant grew slowly but steadily. The food was good, not Michelin Star perhaps but neither were John's prices so people came, had a good meal, enjoyed the atmosphere and seemed to go away happy. The proof always was, would people come back again? And they were starting to. The restaurant was beginning to get its regulars who came in every couple of months or so. And there was always the tourist trade in the summer, whilst not exactly on the coast they were very close and Faversham itself attracted a fair number of day visitors.

Nobody seemed to complain which was always a good sign. That is, until one Saturday lunchtime. John was in the kitchen as usual when he heard a commotion in the restaurant. After a couple of minutes Shirley, one of his two full time waitress' came into the kitchen all flustered. There's a man out there causing a problem saying the food is rubbish and demanding to see the chef. "What did he have?" John asked with a perplexed look on his face,

Shirley said looking at her pad, "He had the steak as far as I can remember, but there was nothing wrong with it."

"I'll go out and see him, don't worry," John said and wiping his hands on his apron went out of the kitchen.

"How you doing 'Coop'?" There standing in the bar area was non other than Jimmy Haynes, a bit fatter and definitely less hair now but you could never mistake him.

"What, what on earth are you doing here Jimmy?" John said in amazement.

Jimmy explained, "Just on holiday over in Herne Bay and had heard about this place and put two and two together with the word on the grapevine that old 'Coop' had started a restaurant. So thought we would come and check it out".

John's face beamed, seeing Jimmy brought back some bad memories but also to some good times. He knew that he owed Jimmy a good deal. "Well, it's good to see you Jimmy, how are you and Brenda?"

"We're fine she's over there with the kids, three now, keeps me on my toes. Good to see you survived, I wasn't sure you would."

John replied earnestly, "Well, that's thanks in no small part to you Jimmy. I hope you haven't paid for your meal because it's on the house, and any other time you come in too."

"I should think so too, food's crap." Jimmy said smiling,

They both burst into laughter, "So, what are you up to now Jimmy?" John asked sitting down on a bar stool next to his old friend.

Jimmy smiled, "Bit of this, bit of that, you know how it is, I do building work now, got to keep the bread on the table with three kids to look after."

John shook his head in disbelief, "Don't tell me you are leading an honest life Jimmy?"

"Hey steady on, I have a reputation to keep." Jimmy grinned and they both shook hands.

John said as he left, "Well, it's good to see you again Jimmy, you take care, and don't forget any time, on the house."

Jimmy waved goodbye, "Thanks Coop', might just take you up on that again, actually the steak wasn't half bad!"

John went back into the kitchen, seeing Jimmy had been good but had stirred up a lot of memories he would rather forget. Shirley came back into the kitchen, "Who on earth was that?"

"Oh, just an old friend from the past." John said wistfully.

Shirley looked quite offended, "Well, John, if you don't mind me saying so, you have some funny friends."

Yes, and you don't know the half of it thought John. "Jimmy is a good man really, you don't have to take any notice of the way he looks."

Shirley sniffed, "Well, he looks to me like he's just come out of prison or something."

John felt his anger rising, "What exactly do you mean Shirley?"

Shirley bridled at John's sudden anger, "Well, he just looks a rough sort, not the sort of person we like in here, that's all."

John turned on her and said, "If you don't like ex-prisoners you better leave then, because that's just where I knew Jimmy from, in prison." John went back into the kitchen and the sound of pots and pans bashing around was there for all to hear.

The next day Shirley didn't come in for work, or the next day, or the day after that. John thought I better make the peace with her so he walked round to her house. He knocked on the door, Shirley answered and looked a bit surprised to see him there. John said, "You haven't been into work for the last few days Shirley, I thought I would check and see if you were ok."

Shirley was quiet for few seconds and took time to answer, "I thought you didn't want me back."

John smiled, "You are my best waitress, if you can bear to work with an ex-con, I would love you to work with me. I am truly sorry I snapped at you, it's just a touchy subject for me."

Shirley, in her usual no nonsense way, said, "Well I better get my hat and coat then and you can walk me into work."

"Friends then?" said John smiling.

Shirley said slapping him on his arm, "Of course you daft bugger." They both laughed and walked down the road together. Shirley slipped an arm through John's as they walked.

****

The restaurant continued to do well and its reputation was growing locally. Around a year after opening John was in his little office at the back of the kitchen one day with Pete his bar manager. He opened a drawer and a folder fell out onto the floor. As Pete picked it up a number of pencil sketches fell out.

Pete looked at them, they were all of a young blonde haired woman with striking eyes. John quickly took the folder from him. During his time in the last prison he had made good use of his artistic training. Prisoners and warders alike used to bring him photographs of wives, girlfriends, children and even their dogs for him to do a portrait.

It was one way of earning a bit of extra cash, or cigarettes, which were as good as money. Plus it gave him a position within the prison community which was liked and respected. The memory that he had once been a police officer seemed now long forgotten, he was a 'con' now like all the others.

But in his spare time he couldn't help but draw from his imagination the most beautiful woman he had ever met. And he didn't find it difficult to recall her features as they seemed etched into his memory for ever.

Pete asked, "Who's the woman then?"

John looked at him wondering how much to say, and decided on very little. "Just someone I knew a long, long time ago, that's all."

"She looks familiar." Pete said.

"I know," replied John. "I think she has one of those faces, the first time I met her I thought I must know her."

"No, really, she looks like the woman in the library in Canterbury," persisted Pete

"I guess my drawings are not that good if they resemble any old person then," said John with a sad smile as he put the folder away.

146

Chapter fifteen

Susan had settled into a routine over the past few years. Work at the library was interesting and with the encouragement of Miss Taylor she had studied part time at Canterbury Christ Church University and had eventually gained a first class honours degree. She was now senior librarian under Miss Taylor and there was every expectation that she would take over when she retired in a few years time.

She loved her little house and spent many happy hours in her small courtyard garden at the rear, growing flowers in tubs and containers of all manner of description. It was a real sun-trap in the evening and Susan loved to sit out in the summer with the newspaper and a glass of wine at the end of a long day.

Life was good, up to a point. Of course there had been a number of men over the years who had tried to gain her attention let alone her affection. And, not to be put off she had been on a number of dates with men, sometimes more than one date. But there seemed to be something holding her back all the time from committing to a full time relationship.

Eventually the men would fall away getting tired of pursuing her without any real reciprocation on her part. It's not that she wasn't attracted to them, in fact some were downright gorgeous but there was an emptiness in her heart and a void that she felt couldn't be filled.

The years she had spent with Steve haunted her, she never wanted to be that dependant upon any man ever again. 'Once bitten, twice shy' was certainly a maxim that she had come to accept. Then, there was always that niggle in the back of her mind about the man she had loved ever so briefly. The man, who had tried to save her, the man who had been responsible for the death of her husband and the man who went to prison to save her name and reputation. Or, at least, that's how she had come to think about it, the fact that it probably was the only way out for him as well was also true but she chose to ignore that fact.

Sally visited in the summer holidays each year bringing the children. At first Susan found her peace destroyed by young children running around and didn't quite know how to cope. But slowly she began to even enjoy their visits as she got to know them and actually grew to love them.

She was their Auntie Sue and they loved to visit and go to the seaside and wild animal parks surrounding the city. Of course, children grow and now when they visited they were young teenage children who tended to either want to lay in bed all day or moan they had nothing to do. Usually a few pounds in their pocket and pushing them out of the door into Canterbury did the trick though.

Sally often asked, "How's the love life then?"

To which question Susan was always a little guarded, "Ok, I guess, I have had a few dates but nothing serious."

Sally understood some of the problem. "You know, not all men are like Steve, you have to give then a chance sometimes. They can be real jerks at times but most don't want to control you to that extent. You got rid of all Steve's belongings including his name. I think that was a smart move to revert back to your maiden name. But you need now to get rid of his hold he still has on you."

Susan knew that Sally usually only said anything if she thought that it was for her benefit and never anything to hurt her feelings intentionally. "I know, I know, it's just that, I don't know." She couldn't bring herself to say the words.

Sally said it for her, "You mean you are still carrying a torch for John Cooper."

The sound of his name spoken out aloud, shocked Susan, "No, no, not really, but yes in a way, I suppose I do compare most men I meet to either Steve or him."

Sally sighed, "You know hun' you really should try and forget him, he went to prison for ten years. Who knows what that will have done to him."

"What do you mean?" Susan asked in a shocked voice.

Sally replied, "Well, you never know, mixing with all those robbers, murderers and drug dealers, it must do something to a man."

Susan looked thoughtful and said,"I had never really given that side of things too much thought, maybe I was trying to avoid it because the thought is too horrible." Susan stared into the middle distance.

"There's another thing," said Sally cautiously, wondering whether she should go any further. But, she had to try and shake Susan out of this way of thinking. "I once read that police officers who end up in prison have a really bad time from the other prisoners, even getting beaten up or worse."

"Oh, don't say that Sally, that's awful." Susan said shaking her head.

Sally tried explain what she meant without upsetting Susan even more. "Well, that could change a man, he could even hate you for involving him and getting him into that."

Susan quickly cut in, "But when I went to see him he told me that he would love me forever."

"What, when was that, you were not supposed to see him," said Sally really surprised.

Susan said, "I know, but I couldn't leave without saying goodbye so I went to the prison just before I left to come down here."

Sally sighed, "Well, that was a long time ago Sue, a lot of water has passed under the bridge since then."

Sally thought, I better change this subject fast before it gets out of hand. "So, tell me about some of the men you have been out with then?"

Susan gave a long sigh, "Well there was Tony recently, here's a photo of us both on the beach at Whitstable."

Sally took the photo and held it up, "Sue he's gorgeous, he looks just like Michael Caine, if you don't want him tell him to come and see me."

Susan slapped her arm, "Sally, stop it, if anybody is happily married that I know it's you."

Sally said, "Maybe, but I could risk it for him". They both rolled about laughing and the atmosphere lifted once again.

Chapter sixteen

The telephone rang in John's office. It was his accountant. "Hello Mr Cooper, this is Tim Bradley from the accountants, I wonder if you could come in to see me in the next day or two, no problem, just that we need to sort out how you are recording invoices and expenditure."

Accounting was not one of John's strong points, but the firm of accountants had come highly recommended so he hoped everything would be ok as the last year's profits, according to his calculations, had been very good.

John caught the train into Canterbury two days later on a beautiful sunny afternoon. He had only been a few time to the city and although not very large he tended to feel more comfortable nowadays in a smaller less crowded place. Canterbury on a summer's day was packed with tourists, many from abroad including coach trips from France.

John made his appointment with the accountant and listened carefully whilst he explained the book keeping procedure he required. John thought, I will need to get someone to do this for me on a regular basis if we are not going to breach any of the tax laws. The last thing John wanted was to end up in any trouble. He had had enough to last him his lifetime.

On the way from the accountant's office John walked past the library on the High Street, he got twenty paces past and the memory of what Pete had said returned to him.

He stopped, I wonder, he thought. No, it was not possible, of all the places she couldn't have settled ten miles from where he had landed. He considered going into the library. There was a seat in a public square so he went and sat in the sunshine to think for a while. What if, just a chance in a million it was her? What would he do? It had been ten years. She could be married with six children for all he knew. He couldn't possibly interfere with her life again if that were the case. Even if she wasn't, how would she greet him? All very well when their affair was still fresh in her mind, but ten years on. She may have changed her opinion altogether and now despise him for killing her husband. When he put it like that it did sound pretty awful, 'killing her husband'.

What to do? Would it do any harm just to satisfy his curiosity by just to popping in and having a look? After all, his memory of her was ten years old, as were his sketches. The person whom Pete had seen could be a much younger person. Yes, that's it thought John, it's a younger version of a similar sort of person. So, I'll just go in and confirm that, so I don't have to think about it anymore.

John walked up the steps. It was an old impressive building unlike many of the more modern libraries. He had read somewhere that it was the first publicly funded library in the country. It seemed to be a mixture of art gallery, museum and library combined. Actually John thought this is not a bad place to spend a couple of hours anyway.

He wandered into the art exhibitions and took a passing interest in the displays. Although he was now an accomplished pencil artist he was by no means an expert on any other form of art, but he enjoyed looking at the works and appreciated the talent that had produced them. He wandered around until he reached the library section. He thought I will just look at a few books and keep myself partially hidden.

He could see the library desk and behind it was a small woman with steel grey hair tied up in a bun. Well, if that's who Pete saw it didn't say much for his drawings. Nevertheless, he kept his head down, sat at a table looking at a photographic book of birds which was only mildly interesting.

Then he heard a voice from the past, he looked over and saw Susan standing over the woman at the desk pointing something out. John's heart stopped and he gasped, she had hardly changed, still as beautiful as ever. Then he heard the woman at the desk say, "Yes, that will be fine Ms Shawcroft. Susan turned and went back into the office. Shawcroft not Denham, did that mean she had re-married. John's spirits sank as fast as they had risen. He got up and walked quickly out. I should never have come in he thought.

All the way home he played that few seconds back in his mind. She was still the same but now belonged to someone else. It didn't dawn on John that old Miss Taylor, in her very particular way of speaking, had referred to Susan as Ms, not Miss as she was a widow but certainly not Mrs Shawcroft.

Fate was playing with them yet again.

Chapter seventeen

Tony arrived at the library with a large bunch of roses. The young library assistants smiled as he walked through. They knew who those were for. He presented them to Susan who was sat at the public desk. "Oh there're beautiful Tony, you really shouldn't waste your money on me."

"Happy birthday Susan," Tony said brightly.

"How did you know it was my birthday?" Susan said smiling and looking over her shoulder at the assistants.

"It pays to know these things about a girl," Tony said, "I thought we might go out for dinner tonight. There's a new restaurant out at Faversham that everybody is talking about, The Jailhouse, that's if you fancy it, or anywhere else really."

Susan thought, why not I have not been out for dinner in ages. "No, the Jailhouse sounds good, I've heard some good reviews about it."

Tony beamed with delight, "Pick you up at seven then."

Tony sat opposite her as they looked over the menu. "What strange names things have, where do they get them from?" Tony read a few of them out, "Seems they all have some sort of Jailhouse connection by the looks of it, goodness knows what's in them. Although I'm sure they don't get too much steak in the prisons out on the Isle of Sheppey".

Pete looked out from the bar of The Jailhouse Restaurant. Well, that's strange he thought, that's the woman from the library I was telling John about. He slipped into the kitchen and told John. "You remember that woman I said looked like your sketches, she is at table 5 with a feller, if you look out you can check the likeness."

John's heart froze, Susan in here, with her husband. No, he couldn't look, why in all the places in the world did they have to be in the same area, what game was fate playing with them. He carried on cooking but after half an hour of fretting, he couldn't resist both another look at Susan and who she was with.

He crept out to the bar area keeping out of the line of sight of table 5. He could see Susan and she looked stunning in a light blue dress and for the occasion she had taken her hair up.

The man sitting opposite was a really good looking man. He would be John thought. He could see them laughing and obviously having a good time. He stayed for a few minutes torturing himself until he could bear it no longer and he went back into the kitchen to take his frustration out on some steaks.

When Susan and Tony had had their meal and left. Pete came into the kitchen and said, "Did you get a look at the woman at table 5."

John didn't look up, "No, I didn't get the time." Just as Pete was turning away he said,"How did they pay, cash or cheque?"

"Cheque, if I remember correctly, yes cheque, I remember ringing it in the till," recalled Pete.

Later that night John went through the till, examining all the cheques from the evenings takings. There was no cheque from anybody called Shawcroft. That's strange thought John, if it wasn't her husband who was it?

Pete had watched John come out of the kitchen and look at the woman. He had noticed John's reaction and was convinced he recognised her. What's all this about he wondered, why be so secretive. He gave it some thought and decided he would give his boss a bit of a push, the woman obviously was the same one and it couldn't be more clear that he thought a great deal of her. The outline of a plan began to form in his mind.

The next afternoon when John was working in the kitchen Pete slipped into the office and took the folder from John's drawer. He removed one of the sketches from the folder. Surely John wouldn't miss one as there were probably in excess of thirty sketches in all. He didn't know if what he intended to do was the right thing, but he liked his boss and he thought that, if it really was the woman in all those pictures, surely a bit of a helping hand to get them together wouldn't hurt. Pete was a bit of a romantic at heart.

On Pete's next day off he went into Canterbury. His usual habit on his day off was to wander around the clothes shops and meet up with a few friends for coffee in one of the many tea shops surrounding the cathedral area.

However, on this occasion he also paid a visit to the library. He went inside and went straight to the cookery section. He chose a book by a well known lady author and slid the portrait into the front of the book but making sure that the top few inches stuck out of the top of the book showing quite clearly when he replaced it on the shelf.

Pete had written the address of the restaurant on the back of the portrait. After he put the book back on the shelf he left quickly without looking at any of the attendants. He didn't want to be remembered. He wasn't quite sure how his plan would work, if at all, but it was worth a try.

His idea was that she should find the sketch and realise that she had an admirer and follow the address on the rear. That was the plan anyway. He didn't feel that he could approach the woman directly. In any case what would he say, "Hey, my boss is sweet on you and has loads of pictures of you." That would be really creepy, enough to put anybody off.

Susan didn't find the picture sticking out of the book, but Miss Taylor did. In her normal fastidious manner she easily spotted a book with paper sticking out, she couldn't have that spoiling the neat look of her shelves.

She examined the sketch, if it wasn't her colleague Susan then it was her double. If it was of her, why was it stuck in a book? Did she have a stalker or something? At that thought she had a shiver go down her spine. She didn't know too many details about Susan's past but little snippets had slipped out over the years, like when she changed her name back to her maiden name. Miss Taylor asked why she would possibly want to do that?

Susan had said quite simply, "There is nothing about my marriage that I want to remember".

Should she mention it to Susan, it was a bit strange? Perhaps she should mention it to her, just so that she could be on her guard at least. She went into the office where Susan was working. "I think you may have a secret admirer," placing the sketch on the desk.

"What's this," said Susan, "where has this come from?"

"It was stuck in a cookery book on the shelf". Miss Taylor said quite sniffily.

Susan turned it over and saw it had the address of the Jailhouse Restaurant on the back. Had someone sketched her whilst she was there a few days ago with Tony? Odd though, because the pose was nothing like anybody sitting in a restaurant and there was something else strange about the drawing.

She stared at it for a while and then it struck her. The hair had been in drawn in long flowing waves over the shoulder like something you would see in a picture of Bridgette Bardot or Raquel Welch. She recalled the style was called a 'bombshell', it looked pretty good and for a moment Susan's mind drifted back. Then it hit her like a bombshell, she had not worn her hair in that style since, since ….1967. What was this all about?

Chapter eighteen

Susan kept the drawing and put it on her mantlepiece. She sat in an easy chair and stared at it for a long time. An uneasy thought process started in her mind. Is there a connection between the restaurant, the picture and her. The restaurant had that odd name of 'The Jailhouse' rather American and the decor fitted it, so was that just a theme or was there more to it. Alternatively, as Miss Taylor had intimated, it could be a stalker. She had had a fair bit of attention over the years in the library and had needed to brush off quite a few advances, some casual but odd ones a little more concerning. The very last thing she wanted in her life was another problem like Steve had become.

What if, she thought, what if, it was something to do with John. Over the years she had not stopped thinking about him but had ceased to wonder if he would ever contact her. Some of the things that Sally had said really worried her. Could there be somebody who goes into the 'Jailhouse' who knew him.

But alternatively, a new terrible thought came into her head, what if it was somebody who knew her ex husband Steve? He did have several cousins, his father was dead, and his mother was a sweet old lady, all of them had very little to do with him whilst he was alive, but you never know. No, they had never bothered her up until now so why should that start. All these contradictory thoughts swam around in Susan's head until it hurt.

She decided the best thing to do was either nothing or make a few enquiries about 'The Jailhouse'. However, her sleep that night was disturbed and many memories invaded her rest, some good but some were terrible and frightening.

The following day whilst she was alone in the office she checked that Miss Taylor and the assistant librarians were all busy in the library and then she made a call to the City Council. "Hi there, I don't know if you can help me, this is Miss Shawcroft from the City Library, we are thinking of doing a display for tourists of local eating establishments. I understand that you keep a register for Food Safety purposes of all the restaurants and eating places in the area. Is it possible for you could send me a list of names, addresses, contact telephone numbers and perhaps owners?"

The man on the other end of the telephone saw nothing unusual in the request. "Yes, sure that information is on public record. I can fax you a copy over this afternoon." Susan put the phone down with a sense of trepidation but also excitement. It's a bit like being a detective she thought.

She flitted about the office all afternoon, she wanted to make sure that when the fax came through she was the only one to get hold of it. She didn't fancy explaining to Miss Taylor, whom she was sure would disapprove of anything which she might consider underhand and a misuse of her position.

Eventually she heard the familiar and unmistakable noise of the fax machine. "I'll get it she shouted across the office." Not that anybody seemed in the slightest bit interested and nobody even looked up. She carefully folded the piece of paper and slipped it into her handbag. All the rest of the day she thought about the piece of paper in her bag, as if it were some sort of living thing in there, waiting to pounce.

At the end of the day she walked home, poured herself a large glass of red wine opened her bag and took out the fax message. Her eyes quickly scanned down the list of restaurants which were in alphabetic order until she came to J.

'The Jailhouse' Restaurant and Bar,
Market Place,
Faversham,
Kent.
Tel: Number - Canterbury 43571,
Owner - Mr John William Cooper.

Susan's heart almost stopped and she gasped. She stared at the paper and the name in front of her. Her hands trembled and her mind was in a whirl. Could it be that after all these years he was within a few minutes of her, alive and well and owning a restaurant she had actually eaten in? The thought was too far fetched to take in all at once.

Then she wondered what to do with this information? Reality was checking in. If it was John who had left the sketch why hadn't he approached her. What was wrong, was he altered in some way? Was it some sort of cruel joke? Maybe Sally would have some ideas, time to talk to her best friend.

Sally listened to it all and said, "Well, bloody hell, where did all that come from." But she continued after her initial shock, "Now listen to me Sue, I want you to go careful here. I know you don't want to hear this but you have to remember what happened last time you two got together. You don't know what he is like now. I can get away this weekend and I want you to promise me that you will do nothing until I get there, promise me."

Susan sighed, "Oh, Sally but if it is him."

Sally was insistent, "No Sue, you have to promise me."

Susan capitulated and said, "Ok, then I promise, but you will come won't you?"

Sally laughed, "Are you kidding, I wouldn't miss this for the world." At last they both laughed.

Chapter nineteen

Sally arrived early Saturday morning and Susan met her at the station. "I have a plan Sue, or at least a bit of one."

"Ok, go ahead I'm all ears," said Susan as she drove back to her house.

Sally said, "First let me go to the restaurant and try and find out if he is there, what he is doing and maybe what he is like now. You never know, he might own the place but live in Nottingham. He might own a chain of Jailhouses, for all we know. How, I have no idea when he has been in prison for ten years, perhaps he learned to rob banks whilst he was in there."

Susan slapped her on the arm in a playful way, "Please Sally don't say that, let's try and keep positive shall we."

Susan looked across at her friend, "Sally, I can't wait, can we go now?"

Sally guessed that this would be the case, "Ok, let's do it, but you must stay in the car until I call you."

They drove straight over to Faversham and parked near the Market Place. "Well, here goes", said Sally. She went into the restaurant and sat at the bar.

Pete approached her. "What can I get you madam."

"How about a coffee and a sandwich," said Sally.

"Sure thing," replied Pete and handed her the bar lunch menu.

Sally screwed up her face as she read the menu, all these silly names just confused her. "If I were to have a toasted 'Bastille' what would that be when it's at home?"

Pete smiled, he was used to this reaction,"That would be French Torchon ham, brie and apple chutney on granary bread."

Sally looked surprised, "Wow, that's a bit more sophisticated than I expected."

"Well, we do out best," smiled Pete eying up Sally, who was still an attractive woman and could turn on the charm when she wanted to.

Pete disappeared into the back with her order and then came back into the bar to organise her coffee. "Do you own this place?" Sally ventured.

"Me, no, I just work in the bar, the boss is in the kitchen." Ok, that's fact number one thought Sally, the boss is here. A few minutes later her sandwich arrived and she tucked into it. To her surprise, it really was very good.

"This is superb actually," she said to Pete, "any chance that I could meet the chef".

"I guess so if he's not too busy." Pete went into the back and came out a couple of minutes later, "Says he'll be out in a minute."

John walked into the bar area wiping his hands on his whites. He saw Sally sitting at the bar but didn't recognise her. In fact they had actually never met before. However Sally recognised him straight away from his photograph in all the local newspapers at the time of Steve's death. "Is everything ok madam?"

Sally looked at him and said, "Well I'm not sure." She flipped the sketch onto the bar. "Can anybody explain this?" Pete went white as a sheet.

John picked up the sketch, "Where did you get this from?"

"It was apparently left in the library." Sally stated in a clipped voice.

John stared at it looking very perplexed, "Well I'm not sure how it got there but this is mine. Who exactly are you?"

Sally said, "I am a friend of the person in that drawing." She looked at John. He looked distressed, but he didn't seem to have altered that much from what she recalled of his photographs. He certainly hadn't put on weight and looked quite fit and trim. There were no tattoos across his forehead or 'love and hate' across his knuckles, so that was a good start.

"What do you want from me?" John said.

Sally looked him straight in the eye and said, "Me, I don't want anything, but there is a lady outside in the car which would like maybe to see you."

"You mean Susan?" said John raising his eyebrows in surprise.

"Yes, of course, who did you think I meant?" said Sally sardonically.

"Won't her husband mind?" John replied somewhat perplexed. Pete tried to look busy wiping glasses, thinking 'my goodness I hope this works out well otherwise I'm out of a job'.

Sally looked confused, "Husband, what husband?"

"Well, I thought she was called Mrs Shawcroft now, she was in here the other night with him?"

Sally shook her head, "You dumb idiot, that's her maiden name, she changed back to it, she's not married, not even thinking about getting married."

"Really, is that true?" said John, his heart missing a beat, "where is she?"

Sally looked at him and thought I really hope I'm doing the right thing here. "She's sitting right outside in a red Mini."

John shot straight out of the restaurant into the street. As soon as he came out Susan saw him and gasped. She jumped out of the car and ran towards him. They didn't say a word but flew into each others arms and kissed. At long last they broke away. "You found me," she said. "I don't know how it happened but we found each other, fate must love us to give us a second chance."

Two woman walked past them and saw John still in his chef whites hugging and kissing Susan. On passing one smiled and said, "If that's the service in this restaurant I'm eating here every week!"

Both Susan and John laughed and walked, arms around each other, back into the restaurant. John looked at Pete, "Is this anything to do with you." Pete just shrugged his shoulders, but the huge grin on his face told it all. "I should fire you."

"I guess you should boss," said Pete.

As they walked past John said in a quiet voice to Pete and Sally, "Thank you."

Within the week John had moved in with Susan into their very comfortable and bijou terraced house in Canterbury. John held Susan in his arms and said, "I loved you before I even knew who you were, I will love you for ever and will never leave you again."

Susan gazed into his face so close now after so many years, "I'm going to hold you to that this time my love"

Chapter twenty
2007

The year is 2007, in the spare bedroom of a small terraced house close to the city centre of Canterbury.

"Grandma, tell me the story again of how you and Grandpa met and how he saved you from the Dragon."

"Ok, but just once more my darling and then you must go to sleep."

Finis

The author spent 32 years as police officer rising to the rank of Chief Superintendent. After taking a BSc(Hons) and an MSc degree in psychology at Sheffield university, he qualified as a chartered psychologist and spent the next 20 years as a consultant psychologist specialising in domestic violence and post traumatic stress disorder. He is now retired and spends his time between sketching, fly fishing and his family. He lives with his wife in Canterbury, England.

OTHER BOOKS BY THE AUTHOR

The Churchwarden's Dog

This is a story of deceit and child abuse perpetrated by those in authority and about an almost perfect murder. It moves away from the ubiquitous lone detective and their sidekick solving murders on their own. Instead we see a small ad hoc mixed group of retired professionals each doing their own thing in a team effort to bring the perpetrators to justice and to expose a cover up of abuse within the Church of England.

The book is set against life in a small Derbyshire Peak District village and one of the main characters is the churchwarden of the village church who becomes the catalyst for the exposure.

This is the first book in a series involving the two main characters.

The Churchwarden and the Haunting of Elsa Gray

This book is a sequel to The Churchwarden's Dog, but it is also a stand alone story. It does, however, bring back some of the main characters using their skills with a new mystery to solve. Once again it is set in a small Derbyshire Peak District market town. Whilst this story is about a ghost it is not really a 'scary ghost story'. Elsa Gray was a young teenager brutally murdered in 1987. For some inexplicable reason her ghost starts to re-appear in the cemetery where she was buried. The church is asked to take an interest and an investigation starts as to why she should appear after so many years.

The investigation naturally revolves around her unsolved murder and as the mystery about her death and the people involved unravels the pace of the story quickens to its final conclusion.

The Churchwarden and the Raven

This is the third book in the Churchwarden Series. A local man, living in the quiet Derbyshire village of Anderton in the Peak District, dies naturally and is cremated. Shortly after, a stranger turns up claiming to be the man who had died. When it transpires that the man they thought they knew for years was really a London ex crime gang member in hiding, things start to get very difficult for Max Webster the Churchwarden. The dead man is believed to have left incriminating evidence hidden somewhere which would do serious harm to the crime gang. As a result organised crime penetrates the quiet sleepy village with murder, kidnapping and blackmail. In this book Sophie Webster comes to the forefront to defend her husband and family, and proves to be a force to be reckoned with.

The Churchwarden and the Ghost

This is the fourth book in the Churchwarden series. Max and Sophie Webster live in a quiet Derbyshire village, or so it seems. There are a number of shadowy figures in the criminal world. One such person was nicknamed the 'Ghost' because he was so elusive and very few people knew who his real identity was. That person was the 'fence' or receiver of high quality stolen goods, mainly gold and jewellery. He could be anybody, but when Max and Sophie Webster have a friend die suddenly in strange circumstances they start to suspect someone who is a member of their village community. Once the secrets start to unravel the story gathers pace with deadly results.

The Dream Team

This is a fast moving psychological thriller set in the city of Sheffield and the Derbyshire Peak District. Dr Jack Hayes is a psychologist specialising in complex trauma cases. Ten years ago he dealt with a number of rape victims perpetrated by a man who has just been released from prison on licence. Jack is disturbed by dreams in which he witnesses the murder of the victims but he has a hard time trying to convince the police that they are in danger and at the same time maintain his professional reputation. That is until they start dying in the same circumstances he predicted. The hunt is then on to prevent more deaths with Jack being pulled more and more into the investigation.

The Shuttle House

Does a house have a soul, certainly some buildings seem to emanate a character and even a presence? Caleb Jackson spots an opportunity to purchase an old house which was built originally to control the water flow to a huge Cotton Mill in the Derbyshire Peak District. He jumps at the chance to modernise it and make it a beautiful place to live in. Even the fact that the old lady who lived in the house before him was labelled as a witch does not put him off.

However, soon after moving into the house strange things start to happen which turns Caleb's life upside down and challenges his scientific and pragmatic view on life. Caleb starts to develop abilities he could never have dreamed possible. Could it be the house?

This is a supernatural murder mystery with a romance thrown in for good measure.

The Shuttle House does in fact exist and it is as described in the story. It really does have a beautiful serene quality to it but, unfortunately, not any magical properties, or at least none that the woman and her dog who live there are admitting to!

A Homecoming of Witches

This is a story about going back, going back home to a place left many years before. Sometimes such moves can evoke wonderful feelings and memories. However, it can also stir up old problems just as easily. When Toby Stafford's wife dies he gives up his job in the police and moves back to live in a small Derbyshire Peak District town. Whilst it had changed over the thirty years he had been away, soon his past starts to catch up with him. When he left as a nineteen year old he didn't realise he was also leaving behind a pregnant girlfriend. His return becomes bound up with an old legend from the town of witch trials in the seventieth century and it all proves that time has a habit of bringing things round to a conclusion. But, it is also a story of lost loves, regained happiness and a coming to terms with grief against a backdrop of families and their personal problems.

The Fire Opal

Bruce Adams' life is going nowhere. He had to take a medical retirement from his job as police detective inspector. Not long after his wife died. He is lonely and depressed with only his dog as a companion. Then one day he finds a ring with a large red gemstone in the woods. The ring once belonged to a man who has been missing without trace for fifteen years. Bruce finds himself reluctantly becoming a private investigator. A missing person turns into a murder enquiry and Bruce's life is turned upside down where not only is the mystery solved but he finds himself, happiness and love again in the process.

A Story for Alice

This is a story told by Tom about his life from boyhood in a poor neighbourhood of a northern town, through to his middle age. He joins the police as a young man and it tracks his progression through the police service which is only marred by his brother's criminal activity. As a result of his brother's stupidity Tom becomes the focus of a psychopathic killer which causes him untold problems over a period of years until its fatal climax.

It is also a story of love lost and regained, of loyalty and sacrifice. It's a story of an honest man's struggle between loyalty to his family and the love of his life. It's not the usual churned out police detective story with a character who seems to have ultimate skills and abilities but a real life person with vulnerabilities, fears and emotions.